SCAVENGERS

stories

SCAVENGERS

stories

BECKY HAGENSTON

University of Alaska Press

FAIRBANKS

Text © 2016 University of Alaska Press

Published by
University of Alaska Press
P.O. Box 756240
Fairbanks, AK 99775-6240

Cover design by Jen Gunderson, 590 Design
Cover images from iStock photo
Interior by UA Press

Library of Congress Cataloging-in-Publication Data
Hagenston, Becky, 1967–
[Short stories. Selections]
Scavengers : stories / Becky Hagenston.
pages ; cm
ISBN 978-1-60223-287-7 (softcover : acid-free paper) — ISBN 978-1-60223-288-4 (ebook)
I. Title.
PS3558.A32316A6 2016
813'.54—dc23

2015022508

For Troy

CONTENTS

I am grateful to the editors of the following publications, where these stories originally appeared:

"The Afterlife" *Bellingham Review*

"Scavengers" *Indiana Review*
           reprinted in *Surreal South 2013* (Press 53)

"Arctic Circus" *The Threepenny Review*

"Puppet Town" *Moon City Review*

"Good Listener" *Black Warrior Review*
           reprinted in *24 Bar Blues: Two Dozen Tales of Bars, Booze, and the Blues* (Press 53)

"The Lake" *Hobart*

"Secrets of Old-Time Science Experiments" *Cold Mountain Review*

"Ivy Green" *Passages North*

"Crumbs" *Freight Stories*

"Let Yourself Go" *The Cincinnati Review*

"Cool" *One Teen Story*

"Hilda" *The Chattahoochee Review*

ACKNOWLEDGMENTS

My sincere thanks to the friends who supported me with encouragement and good advice as I wrote these stories: Joyce McMahon, Michael Kardos, Catherine Pierce, Rich Lyons, Holly Johnson, Kate Ledger, Cathleen Keenan, Lynda Majarian, Margo Rabb. Thanks to Rich Raymond, department head extraordinaire, and to my colleagues at Mississippi State University. Thanks to James Engelhardt, Amy Simpson, Krista West, and everyone at University of Alaska Press, and to Joeth Zucco for such eagle-eyed copy editing. Thanks to my sister, Cindy Perdue, for giving me great advice—editorial and otherwise. I am grateful for a scholarship to the Summer Literary Seminars in St. Petersburg, Russia. Thanks to my parents and in-laws for being wonderful. Thanks to Benjamin Percy for choosing *Scavengers* as the winner of the Permafrost Book Prize in Fiction.

Thanks most of all to my husband, Troy DeRego, for your love, unwavering support, and stories about bats.

The Afterlife

It's ten weeks since her husband's accident, two days since she arrived in St. Petersburg. The late June sun is shining high in the marbled blue sky as it has since just past three in the morning when Connie was awakened by loud voices on the sidewalk below her window. She had peered down to see a group of laughing boys carrying cans of Baltika beer; they turned left toward Nevsky Prospekt and Connie lay back on her hard twin-sized bed and tried to go back to sleep. Now she is in the Amber Room of the Catherine Palace, and Sergei the tour guide is saying something about the Nazis stealing it. How do you steal a whole room? she wonders, and then the corners of her eyes are going gray, the jeweled walls turning dusky, her ears filling with cotton. She knows this feeling; she had it when she got food poisoning as a young girl; she had it ten weeks ago when the uniformed police officer came to her door. As soon as she realizes what's about to happen, she's on the floor. She stares up at Sergei, who is leaning over her, saying something soothing, his glasses perched on the end of his nose. Then she tilts up her head and kisses him on the mouth.

It isn't the kiss that troubles her—that could be dismissed, laughed off. *I was dizzy*, she might say, if she ever tells this story. *I hadn't slept. I hadn't eaten. I was confused.* But she hasn't mistaken Sergei's face for her husband's, and she doesn't care that everyone— the tour group, the babushka who guards the room—is watching. It's as if she's turned into someone else entirely, someone who is in love with Sergei, someone who—even after registering his bemused expression—knows with a stunning clarity: *This is the best thing that will ever happen to me.*

On the fifteen-mile bus ride back to the city, she sits in the last row and leans her head against the window. Up front, in the seat behind the driver, Sergei is quiet, though he does get on the PA system once to announce that the bus for Peterhof will leave on Sunday at 7:30 a.m. and to meet in the lobby of the mini hotel at 7:20.

Some of the other tourists look at her with concern, and a sixtyish woman in red-framed glasses walks to the back of the bus and offers her a warm bottle of Pepsi. The familiarity of the Pepsi—the logo recognizable even in Cyrillic—is somehow a disappointment. "No, thanks," Connie says. "I feel okay now that I've eaten." Then she closes her eyes, and when she opens them the woman is gone.

When she gets off the bus, Sergei says, "Take care now," and smiles at her, and she nods and coughs and walks quickly into the hotel.

That evening, she calls Diane, her mother-in-law, from her cell phone, even though she knows it will cost eight dollars a minute. Diane says, "Oh my goodness," when Connie informs her that she fainted in the Catherine Palace. "Are you okay?" There's a strange lilt to her voice, as if she's pleased by this news. As if, Connie realizes, she's hoping Connie might be pregnant. Which she most certainly isn't.

"It was because I skipped breakfast," Connie says, omitting the part about kissing the tour guide. "And a few hours later I got dizzy and fainted. Up until then I was having a great time, though." This is true. She had taken a photo of a statue of Pushkin, even though she was fuzzy on who exactly he was. And the Catherine Palace was as her guidebook depicted: birthday-cake blue with golden spires, Roman-looking statuary romping across topiary gardens. She had skated across the ballroom floor in blue paper booties. "The tour guide was very nice, got me orange juice and took me to the cafeteria. I mean, he took all of us there, not just me." Sergei's glasses had almost fallen off when she kissed him, and his breath tasted like lemon. If he's thinking of her now, is he thinking in English or Russian?

"I'm glad you're okay," Diane says. "I hope you're taking lots of pictures to show me and Jeffrey when you get home."

"Oh, yes. Lots."

"His appetite is better. Turns out he wants Cookie Crisp for every meal, though— remember that cereal? He used to love that, as a little boy. I only bought it on special occasions, though. Too much sugar."

Outside Connie's window, a drunk man is curled up on the sidewalk. A black-and-white cat makes its way over to him, sniffs him, and then marches on. It's ten thirty at night, and the sun is still shining. It won't set for another two hours.

"It's ten thirty and the sun is shining," Connie says. "I feel like should do something. I think I'll go for a walk."

"Be careful. I'll tell Jeffrey you send your love. Now." She pauses for so long that Connie wonders if they've been cut off. "You're sure you're okay?"

"Positive," Connie says. "It was low blood sugar, that's it."

"I'll tell Jeffrey you send your love," Diane repeats, before saying good-bye.

Connie imagines Jeffrey blinking at his mother, asking, *Who?*

But she's far away from all that, Connie reminds herself. What does a person do in a place where the sun never sets? A group of young people are walking up the sidewalk with the ubiquitous blue cans of Baltika, laughing uproariously. She watches them sidestep a bum and continue toward Nevsky Prospekt. She can hear the noise of Nevsky from here, two streets over—all those horns honking. Russians drive like lunatics. She'd thought drivers were crazy back home in Baltimore, but they're absolutely nuts here.

It's Wednesday, and she is here for six more days. The day before yesterday, she had flown over the Alps; she had eaten the Lufthansa cheese sandwich and craned out the window at the snowy peaks and tried not to think of Jeffrey in his windowless hospital bedroom, watching cartoons.

In the lobby, Connie drops her key off with a sour-looking woman behind the desk, different from the sour-looking woman she had retrieved her key from this afternoon. She's seen these babushka women all over the city, sweeping the streets and sitting sternly in the rooms of the Catherine Palace. Connie musters a smile. "*Speceeba*," she says, but the woman makes no response, and Connie wonders if she pronounced it wrong.

On the way out, she nearly collides with two people she recognizes from the tour bus—a Birkenstock-wearing Australian man who is tanned a dark khaki and a tiny, pale woman with deep red lipstick. Connie had assumed she was French for some reason, but when she speaks she has a thick, southern accent.

"How're yew feeling?" she asks, and places her hand on Connie's arm. Both she and the man are dressed up, the woman in a bright red dress and a shawl, he in a suit and Birkenstocks.

"Oh, I'm just fine," Connie says. How many people had witnessed her kissing the tour guide? How long would people keep asking if she was okay? You can only say it so much—*I'm fine, really. I'm hanging in there, I promise. I'll be okay.* You can only say that so many times before you want to get on a plane and go someplace where no one knows you.

"We were just at the ballet," the Australian man says. "*Sleeping Beauty.* It was beautiful. They'll get you tickets to the Mariinsky if you ask at the desk."

"Okay," says Connie, and waves at them as they disappear into the hotel. She stands on the sidewalk. Someone has covered the sleeping bum with a newspaper. The heat of the day is just beginning to disappear. If she turns right, she will get to the Cathedral of Our Lady of Kazan, with its huge curved colonnades. She hasn't been inside a church since her wedding, and that was only because Jeffrey had insisted. She had wanted to get married in Vegas.

She passes the cathedral and then she's walking down Nevsky, still busy this time of night. A one-legged man in a drab green army uniform is sitting on a blanket next to a hot dog cart (she thinks they're hot dogs), saying, "*Pomegetye, pazhalsta, pomegetye.*" She knows *pazhalsta*—please—but she doesn't know the other word. Money, perhaps?

All the women are wearing high heels; they look like tramps, thighs and midriffs bared. They look like high-class prostitutes, and it occurs to her that maybe some of them are. They walk stony faced, chatting on cell phones. A group of boys in leather jackets pass by her; she pulls her purse closer. One of the things the guidebooks warned you about were pickpockets.

She walks until she can see the yellow-and-turquoise domes of the Church on Spilled Blood, rising against the fading sky, and she stares at it as she joins the crowd of people crossing Nevsky. The sun is going down, and the clouds are turning pale gray. The vendors selling *matryoshka* dolls and Soviet hats have packed up their booths. The church is on the place where Alexander II was literally blown to pieces, an elaborate version of a cross by the side of the road. Connie is standing on a bridge over a canal, an offshoot of the Neva River. She left her guidebook back at the hotel, and now she wishes she had it with her. She wants to locate herself.

A man approaches with a portfolio of drawings and says to her in English, "You wish to buy?"

She shakes her head and walks away, wondering how he knew she was a foreigner, how she had been so easily found out.

The next morning she sits with the red glasses woman at breakfast. She'd wanted to skip breakfast altogether. She'd wanted to find a supermarket and buy some cheese and bread, but when she woke up she had such a headache from not sleeping that she decided she'd better risk the awkwardness of small talk with strangers and brave the dining room. She'd been almost relieved when she saw the red glasses woman waving her over to her table.

"You had quite a spill yesterday," the woman says. "How are you feeling?"

"I'm really fine. It was just low blood sugar."

The woman gives her a coy, amused look. "Sergei is quite a doll, isn't he?" She raises her eyebrows, as if waiting for Connie to tell her a secret.

"I guess," Connie says. "I didn't notice." She rubs her temple. "I couldn't sleep last night," she says, hoping to change the subject.

"Mosquitoes!" the woman says. "Oh, I know. I had to spray repellent all over myself. Do you need some repellent? I have extra. I always pack extra, just in case."

"I have some," Connie says. "It wasn't the mosquitoes. I think I'm just not used to the time change." Actually, she had lain awake all night thinking of Sergei, wondering how she could get him to kiss her again. What on earth was the matter with her?

"Hmm," says the woman. "Is that so?" She has a prying, grandmotherly way about her. Connie had never known any of her grandparents, and they probably never knew she existed.

"My name's Rita," says the woman, extending a hand.

Connie introduces herself. The dining room has become considerably louder since she sat down; a group of tourists from France is conversing in near-hysterical tones. She has to say her name twice for Rita to catch it.

"So, Connie, what brings you here to Russia?"

"I don't actually know," Connie says, staring intently at her blinis. The waitress is bringing around tiny cups of coffee, but she seems to be avoiding their table.

"Ooh, that is the *best* reason to go someplace!" Rita cries, clapping her hands like a child. "I always think that if you don't *have* a reason, if you just go—well, then a place can change you. You don't have expectations getting in your way, you see."

"Huh," says Connie. But what if your only expectation is to be changed? she wonders, and decides not to ask.

"But why Russia? Of all the places in the world?" Rita is staring at Connie with wide, unblinking eyes. Connie feels a flash of annoyance: Haven't they just established that not having a reason was reason enough? "I have Russian heritage, you see," Rita goes on. "My grandmother once saw the little grand duchesses waving from the windows of the imperial train. Such a tragedy." She shakes her head. "My grandmother had many stories about her life in St. Petersburg. And then in Petrograd and Leningrad! Oh, I'll tell you all about it." She reaches across the table and pats Connie on the hand.

Connie feels desperate for coffee. She says, "Excuse me?" but the waitress whisks by without stopping. She sighs. "Me, too," she says to Rita. "Russian heritage, I mean. My great-grandfather." Because who knew, really? It could very well be true.

If only there was a full-color guide to her life, with starred attractions and pertinent history. Is that too much to wish for? Her past isn't nearly as complicated as the history of St. Petersburg, not nearly as full of bones and martyrs and false prophets and tragic decisions. But also not nearly so full of art and literature and music and beauty, she supposes, staring at her full-color guide in the long line to the Winter Palace, balancing her umbrella against the crook of her arm.

This would be her full-color guide: begin with a baby picture that, as far as she knows, doesn't exist; move on to the red-brick house where Aunt Caroline lived, then the ambulance that took her body away and the cop car that took away Uncle Frank; turn the page to see the Brown family (was that their name?) and then the Maxwells, the Freemans, the Riches, the Comptons, the Greens, the Baxters. The white car from Social Services. Another brick house, another brick school.

She glances up from under her umbrella to see if the line to the entrance of the Hermitage is moving yet. She would have gotten here sooner, but it had taken almost an hour to extricate herself from Rita, who was intent on asking personal questions. "And where was your great-grandfather from?" she demanded. "What was his last name? Are you married? What's *your* last name?"

"I need to go to the bathroom," Connie said. She had taken her purse and not gone back to the breakfast table.

"Aren't you curious?" Jeffrey had asked, when she told him about her family—or rather, her lack of a family. She had told him about growing up in foster homes, leaving out most of the grisly details, because who needed grisly details on a third date? Or ever?

She and Jeffrey met at the middle school where she taught geometry. She had thought he was a father, waiting in the school office to retrieve his child, and had given him a noncommittal smile. Later, she admitted that she'd felt jealous of the woman he was married to, and for their no-doubt gorgeous children. She asked, "Who are you waiting for?" and he said, "I'm supposed to meet the superintendent to talk about my design for the Media Center." When the superintendent didn't show up, he invited her to get a cup of coffee, and that was that. Their trajectories had met and melded and formed one straight, shimmering line into the future. He drew this on drafting paper, the line lofting over a house and off the page.

In a dim pub in Fell's Point, he told her about growing up with a mother but no father, and then they talked about the family they would make together, the two boys and a girl, or the one boy and two girls—the five of them, living in the house they would build together by the Chesapeake Bay.

She could imagine all of this so clearly that it was as if it had already happened, a memory in reverse. Even now, standing in a snaking line in the rain in front of the pale green expanse of the Winter Palace, she can almost remember the things that didn't happen and never will: the children, the swing set on the lawn, the Christmas ornaments being chased across a thick carpet by a Labrador retriever puppy. "Perhaps you've mistaken us for a decorative plate from the Franklin Mint?" Jeffrey said, when she told him about the puppy and the ornaments.

But she could just as easily imagine the kids crying in the closet and the Christmas tree falling on the carpet and herself pounding her hand against the wall until she made a hole, and Jeffrey saying, "Who the hell did I marry?" Not that she told him this. Surely, she thought, real life must be somewhere in between.

He proposed after three weeks, when she was so in love her body seemed to glow and buzz when he touched her. "Vegas," she said. And he said, "My mother would kill me."

You would expect a mother to be the voice of reason about such things, but apparently Diane didn't see anything wrong with Connie and Jeffrey getting married six weeks after their first date, as long as it was in a church. "When you know, you know," she told Connie, and patted her on the cheek.

The Hermitage is so full of tourists that Connie keeps finding herself squashed in doorways, trapped between tour groups. She cranes her neck, her heart galloping, wondering if Sergei is here, if he's leading a group through the marbled hallways. She tells herself she's looking for masterpieces, but she can't get close enough to any of the paintings for a good look, so finally she gives up and sets about finding a room where she can breathe. In the guidebook photos, the halls and marble staircases are empty, no baffled tourists clotting the corridors, blocking the view of the Cézannes, no tour guides waving umbrellas or artificial flowers above their heads. Sergei could be here somewhere, or he could be out in the world, buying black bread, eating lunch, perhaps thinking of her. The thought makes her chest feel hollow and carbonated.

She pushes through the people, past the tour guides—none of them Sergei—and the tourists, through rooms of important paintings she can't see because of the crowds, and finds herself at last in a vast hall of golden pillars. There's a strange silence; no clumps of tourists here. The inevitable babushka is scowling in a corner, making sure no one touches anything. Connie sits down on a red velvet bench and takes out her guidebook.

She's in the Armorial Hall. In 1914, she reads, the Winter Palace was converted into a hospital, where the Empress and her two eldest daughters nursed the wounded. Connie closes her eyes, but she can't imagine it or even believe it. She looks at the crystal chandeliers high above her—the same chandeliers dying soldiers stared at as the Empress changed their bandages? A woman and a boy sit on the bench next to hers and talk quietly in Spanish, poring over a map. After a moment they get up and walk away. If Sergei were here, he could tell her what everything means. The guidebook can't bring the past to life; it just buries it further. All that seems real to her now is her stomach growling and the sweat gathering beneath her armpits.

On her search for the exit, she finds herself in a long corridor filled with paintings of tsars and tsarinas staring down from gilded frames—some dour, as if they know what's coming; some arrogant, as if they don't care. She has started from the wrong direction, the end of the Romanovs: Nicholas, with his impossibly sweet eyes; Alexandra, flint eyed and strawberry blonde; and their gorgeous, doomed children.

Peter the Great is last—or first, if she'd started from the right direction—stern and handsome (could he have really been that handsome?) and warrior-like, standing before a dark, ashy background that looks like the beginning of the world, or maybe the end.

How do you get through the day when night never comes? At home, she'd been going to bed before the sun set, but here she finds herself longing for the half light of two and three in the morning. She naps throughout the day and wakes at midnight to eat the cheese and bread she purchased from a grocery store called, for some reason, Dixie, and then she sets out walking. She watches the sun sink into the Neva. She follows chattering, drunken boys and girls across bridges and canals. So many bridges! A wedding party lounges on the Anichkov Bridge—with its giant statues of men taming wild horses—drinking from Baltika cans, laughing. The bride is wearing a dress as frothy as icing. Connie has seen these wedding parties throughout the city, taking photos against the backdrop of the Neva, drinking and shouting. Sometimes she thinks she sees Sergei among them, but she's never entirely sure.

She never told Jeffrey this, but after their cup of coffee in the school, she had left work early, claiming illness, and followed him. She watched him half-walk, half-jog to his car. She followed him to his office park and sat there in her car, her heart pounding as if she had already lost him. She followed him to his apartment and parked by the curb, wondering what to do, feeling like a fool. Even then she knew it was crazy. The next day he called her, and she wept with relief as soon as she hung up.

Now, she feels that familiar, welcome surge of shame and panic as she wanders the streets of St. Petersburg in the dim light, imagining Sergei everywhere: on Bankovksy Bridge, beside the golden griffins. Smoking a cigarette outside the Literary Café. Walking down the Palace Embankment. Jogging across the traffic around St. Isaac's Square, as if to outrun her.

In the first days and weeks after the accident, Connie felt like a ghost, manifesting in places without knowing how. She'd be standing there in the Safeway staring at cereal—Jeffrey liked Grape Nuts—and then she'd be at home, in her kitchen, sobbing and holding two grocery bags. Sometimes she found herself at the school with no memory of getting there, and she'd have to go outside and locate her car in the parking lot.

She was given a leave of absence—her teaching assistant would handle things—but she could tell the principal preferred her to stay working. After all, there wasn't going to be a funeral. "You must be so relieved," people said to her. "What a blessing," they said. "What a miracle."

She visited Jeffrey in the hospital, fed him applesauce with a spoon. He clutched her fingers like an infant. He smiled as if he almost knew her. The doctor and nurses told her that he might start to remember some things, but it would take time, and he would never remember her as his wife. "He'll remember you as the nice lady who comes to visit him." Even his body was taking on the soft contours of a child, all those years at the gym melting away, the thirty-mile bicycle rides. He was the ghost of her husband, turning back into Diane's little boy.

But there were times when she swore he *did* remember her—or almost. She could see the struggle, see him wavering between worlds.

"Of course you'll get a divorce," Diane told her. "No one expects you to stay married. You'll meet someone else, maybe you'll have children." She said this while stroking Jeffrey's hand, and it seemed to Connie as if she was speaking only to him, as if her words might guide him back from wherever he'd gone.

On Saturday, Connie is awoken by a shriek and the pounding of feet in the hallway. She hears Rita's voice, high and hysterical: "My passport!" More feet pounding, doors opening and slamming. Rita's voice again: "I don't *know*."

It's one in the afternoon. When Connie gets downstairs to the lobby, she feels like she's wandered into an Agatha Christie novel: Seven people are fidgeting in a row of chairs while a tall blonde woman from the front desk stalks back and forth in front of them, her hands clasped behind her back.

"What happened?" Connie says to no one in particular.

Rita stares at her with desperate eyes. "Oh, Connie, the most terrible thing. My passport was stolen! I don't even know when it happened; it could have been days ago. I was just looking for it now because I wanted to exchange money, and it's gone."

"You should have left it in the safe," says the blonde woman, eyeing them all like they're murder suspects.

"Actually, the best thing is to just have it with you at all times," says Birkenstock man. He lifts up his shirt to reveal a wallet strapped to his tanned chest.

"I'm supposed to fly home in two days!" Rita says. "This is terrible!"

"We will report to the police, and then you will go to the consulate," the woman tells her. "Is big problem." She shrugs. "You should have kept it in the safe. You will not leave in two days."

Rita starts to sob, and Connie turns and heads back up to her room to see if she's been robbed as well. But no, there's her passport, tucked into the inside pocket of her suitcase, still in its hanging wallet. It's almost a disappointment to see it there. Connie's own face—nine years younger, staring eagerly toward a trip to Italy that never materialized—feels like a betrayal. Who was she, that younger self, to think she had so much to look forward to? Italy had been the idea of a boy from college. He'd said it in jest, she realized later, *We should go to Italy together and eat real pizza.* But she had thought, Yes, of course we should!

Six weeks ago, she had remembered that passport, the one she thought she would need when she and Jeffrey went on their honeymoon in Europe. (Then it turned out he wanted Hawaii. Who knew? Not that they'd gone there, either. "We'll save our honeymoon for our first anniversary," he'd told her.)

"I need to go away," she said to the travel agent, a woman with soft, sad brown eyes and a poster of Tahiti behind her. It was hard to find travel agents anymore; everything was done online. But she wanted to talk to someone. "My husband was killed."

The travel agent said, "Oh no, I'm so sorry!"

"I need to go someplace far," Connie said. "Someplace where I can't read the alphabet. Someplace where I can feel lost for a while, but not a jungle or anything. I don't want to be in physical danger. I just want to be far away from everything that seems familiar. Do you understand?"

The travel agent nodded. "You'll need a visa."

"Good," said Connie.

It's comforting, having her passport close against her body. She can feel it sticking to her stomach as she perspires, walking in the hot sun across Troitsky Most, a bridge that is much longer than it first seemed. She is going to the Peter and Paul Fortress—"built on the bones of forced laborers," according to her guidebook. Prisoners languished in airless cells there for hundreds of years, but now the beach is strewn with sunbathers and swimmers who are unafraid of the Neva's infected waters.

The Cathedral of St. Peter and St. Paul is too small for so many tourists. She has to literally elbow a woman in the ribs to get close enough to snap a picture of the small, separate chapel where Tsar Nicholas and Alexandra are interred, along with three of their five children and four servants who were shot with the family. A woman standing too close behind her is saying, "How tragic, what a tragedy," and Connie wants to say, "Well, what isn't?" but instead she extricates herself from the gawking throng and wanders past the tombs of Catherine the Great and Peter the Great, and Alexander Somebody—not Great. It takes her almost ten minutes to squeeze her way back to the exit. If a fire broke out everyone would be crushed to death; everything would burn except the marble tombs.

But what does that matter, she wonders, as she stumbles into the sunshine. Someone could come along and tell her there are no Romanovs at all in those marble tombs; there never was a Last Tsar and his doomed family. The dead are unreachable, and this is as close as any of the living can ever get to them. You have to make them up; you have to read stories about them that might not even be true.

She had no interest whatsoever in finding her birth parents, but she knew that Jeffrey wanted a different story, so she told him she had tracked them down when she was in her early twenties. "They were glad to hear from me," she said. "They lived in Virginia and gave me up because they were so poor. Two years after I found them, they were killed in a fire." She felt a little bad, killing off her nonexistent mother and father, a kindly couple who wanted only the best for her.

At one of the Fortress gift shops, she buys a booklet about the Romanovs, deliberately choosing an edition in Russian so she can't read anything except the looks on the imperial family's faces.

The next day is Sunday, and Sergei will be in the lobby at 7:20. Connie had slept fitfully, as usual, and got up at four, suddenly parched, scooping water out of the sink before she remembered it was poisonous. You weren't even supposed to brush your teeth with it. She had three full bottles of fizzy water, but no—she had drunk from the parasitic Neva. She lay back down, waiting for what she had coming to her, but apparently nothing was coming. By seven she is feeling pathetic, afraid, and perfectly healthy. She eats breakfast by herself, pretending not to see Rita in the breakfast room, but Rita spies her.

"Going to Peterhof with us?" she asks. All panic from the previous day seems to have vanished.

"Did you find your passport?" Connie asks, and Rita's face clouds.

"No, I didn't," she says. "I went to the police department yesterday and filled out some paperwork. I'm going to the consulate tomorrow, and thank goodness I can stay in my room for a while longer. It might take a week! I have to rebook my tickets!" She pats Connie on the arm as if to reassure her that it's not her fault. "But let's not think about that now. There's Peterhof to look forward to. You know, when my grandmother was young, she saw the little duchesses on the imperial train. She said they were adorable."

"So there's worse things than losing a passport," Connie agrees. "There's getting shot to death with your family."

Rita stands up, as if she's been personally insulted. "The bus is waiting," she says, and stalks off.

She doesn't think Sergei is actually ignoring her on purpose; he just seems to have forgotten everything that happened at the Catherine Palace: the fainting, the kissing. She shoves herself to the front of the small crowd of fellow tourists, trodding on a foot and eliciting a "Hey!" from its owner. They are wearing, once again, blue paper booties and standing in another impossibly gilded ballroom. Sergei leads them through room after elaborate room, past paintings of Catherine with her little dog, through bedchambers and sitting rooms, explaining that the Grand Palace was destroyed in World War II and that rooms were still being restored.

"Fascinating," hisses Rita, close behind Connie. "Don't you think?"

Connie ignores her. She moves up closer to Sergei, wondering if there is something she can say to make him remember what happened last week. Should she faint again? But then they are outside in the fresh air, removing their booties, depositing them in trash cans. She is standing on the terrace, staring at the Grand Cascade: fountains as far as she can see, golden men reaching toward each other.

"Peter the Great wanted a palace to rival Versailles," Sergei announces, over the sound of the fountains and the shouts ofother tour guides, other groups. "And as you can see, he accomplished it!"

"I have never been to Versailles," Rita says in Connie's ear. "Have you?"

"Yes," Connie lies. "It's just like this."

The group is breaking into clumps and pairs, wandering off in search of snacks and toilets. Sergei calls, "Remember you need five rubles for the toilets!" like a mother reminding her kids to take their lunch money. Rita has squeezed next to him and is gazing up in an embarrassing way. "My grandmother saw the little grand duchesses on the imperial train," she says. "Did you grow up here in St. Petersburg, born in Leningrad? Did your parents or grandparents survive the Siege?"

Sergei has put on sunglasses and is staring toward the Gulf of Finland. "I am from here," he says, and he starts walking away, down the terrace, but Rita scampers after him, calling, "But what's it *like*? To have grown up surrounded by such *history*?"

Oh, God, it's too awful. Connie has to stop her. She walks fast, inserts herself between the old woman and Sergei, and says, "I actually have a question."

Sergei turns to her. She can't see his eyes, but his eyebrows seem furrowed. "Yes?"

"Those men on Nevsky Prospect, begging. They're saying *pazhalsta* something. Something like *pomegranate*, but not that."

"*Pomegetye*," says Sergei. "It means 'help.'" And then he sets off walking fast, too fast for Rita with her short legs. Connie and Rita both watch him descend the Grand Terrace, passing the golden fountain of Samson wrestling a lion.

Help, please. What would it be like, to stand—or sit—on the sidewalk all day, saying those words over and over to anyone who will listen and anyone who won't? Help. Please.

"Are we walking together?" Rita asks Connie brightly. Sergei has become a distant speck, moving among the water and the statues.

Connie realizes she is shaking. She's thinking about being in her car in traffic, two years before she met Jeffrey, and following a man's red Jeep, passing to try to get closer, crashing into a convertible.

She had not tried to explain or even understand the tether that pulled her, the imaginary—she knew it even then—lasso that reached from her heart to . . . well, to nothing, really. She gave fake insurance information to the sorority girl she'd collided with, not because she wanted to avoid paying, but because she wanted to avoid being reminded of what an idiot she was. The man she was following was someone she hardly knew; they had met at a bar. He had given her his number and she had called, and he hadn't called back.

"No," Connie says to Rita. The sweat is running down her back. She takes out her sticky passport wallet from inside her shirt and wears it out, around her neck. Rita looks at it as if it's something Connie is using to taunt her with, and Connie feels a twinge of pity for the old woman—and for herself. And for Diane, thousands of miles away, feeding Jeffrey with a spoon, telling him that Connie sends her love.

And then she walks, in the blue-skied heat, as fast as she can, in the green grass along the canal toward the Gulf of Finland. She passes the others from her tour group; she passes Sergei; she passes golden fountains, fishes, and gods. She is drenched in sweat by the time she gets to the small sandy beach, and then she just keeps walking, until the earth ends.

The water is colder than she'd expected. Then, as she keeps moving, the coldness seems to dissipate, dissolved by the warmth of her own body. She's an excellent swimmer. She can swim all the way to Helsinki if she has to. She leans her body forward, ducks under water, and begins to stroke and kick, and when she stops she can't touch the bottom. Too late she realizes that her passport has floated right off her neck.

There will be complications now. A trip to the consulate tomorrow with Rita, of all people. The two of them waiting on benches in hallways, faxes back and forth to America, phone calls and rescheduling, photos and signatures and forms. There's no telling how long it will take to get things sorted out. She will have to hear all of Rita's stories about her grandmother and the grand duchesses; she will learn where Rita is from, her history, and why she's never seen Versailles. Connie might tell more lies about herself, or she might tell some of the truth.

She treads water and watches a hydrofoil lofting across the water, making its way toward Helsinki. She lifts a hand and waves; she can see people waving back. Now she knows what missing Jeffrey feels like, and will possibly always feel like: the water beneath her, this endless floating.

When snow begins to fall on the Gulf of Finland and darkness creeps into St. Petersburg from all directions, she will be home, in America. She won't be here when the Neva turns to ice; she will miss the long Russian winter. Sometimes, when she's talking to Jeffrey, she'll be thinking about the tourists skating on their paper slippers over ballroom floors, as if they're at a party that no one among the living can remember.

SCAVENGERS

On the game show, Margaret veered from the script and did not say, "Yes, I'm married to my wonderful husband, Donny." In response to the exuberant host's note-carded question—"And it says here you've been married for eight years?"—Margaret looked straight at the camera and said, "No, Chip, you're mistaken." Then, unable to stop herself, she practically shouted, "Everything I win is all mine!"

Then they were on to the next contestant, married for thirteen years to his beautiful wife, Barbara, and the next, a chubby red-headed girl who collected insects and had come "all the way from Kansas City." By the time the show aired a week later, Margaret couldn't bear to watch herself lose to the insect girl, and, even worse, she had decided not to leave Donny after all.

Back home in Mississippi he was a dental hygienist, and he hadn't gone with her to the taping because he had to hose out the mouths of root canal patients. "Why not just go ahead and be a dentist?" she had asked him on their first date, and he said, "You go ahead and be a dentist." Not that she could make fun of him now, because he had a job and she didn't.

"Everything I win is all mine," Donny called from the living room, where he was watching the program even though she told him not to. "That's funny."

The game show, the game show, the game show! She lay in bed after Donny had gone to work and tried to will herself back there, back to California and the studio lot and the palm trees, the green room and the makeup people and the studio audience who had seemed to genuinely care so much about her. When she asked for a *D* and there was no *D* on the board, a loud AWWW echoed around her, and she felt cradled in support and goodwill. Maybe that's what church was supposed to be like, but at church she'd always felt itchy and only read the bulletin to find typos. *Our Lard in Heaven, Here my Prayer!* That was the best one.

On the phone to her mother in Memphis, she said, "They were so nice backstage after I lost. Chip shook my hand, and his assistant Julianna gave me a hug."

"What was that about not being married?" her mother said.

"I was joking. We're encouraged to joke."

"Oh," said her mother, who watched nothing but infomercials.

"If we're funny, we might get invited back." No one had told her this, but it sounded plausible. "Or maybe some talent scout will watch and think, Oh, I need this person in my reality show."

"Who needs a reality show?" her mother said. "Real life is real enough."

"True," said Margaret. "It's plenty real all right."

Would it hurt or help her chances if there were children? She
up the camera in her living room, in front of the open window
that revealed the springtime lawn of the front yard. The magnolia
tree hid the trashy house across the street with the rusty swing
set and dilapidated picnic table in the yard. Margaret and Donny
had been meaning to move for five years now but hadn't gotten
around to it.

If she wanted to be on that show where they swapped wives,
she would need children. It was called *Wife Swap*, but really it
was about putting the Redneck Woman in a household full of
little liberal Poindexters, and the Professor Wife in a trailer filled
with shotgun-carrying hillbilly children. That didn't seem fun to
Margaret. She didn't know if she could survive in the wild or eat
bugs, but maybe she could. *Would you rather live with a bunch of
hillbilly children or eat bugs?* she tweeted. She liked tweeting, she
liked having followers. There were over five hundred of them now,
and she didn't know who any of them were. After she lost on the
game show, she tweeted, *O the agony of defeat*, which wasn't clever
but it expressed how she felt, and GrlPwr3 wrote, *You rock n dont
forget it!!!!!!* Many of her followers did not spell correctly, but she
didn't let it bother her much.

BUGZ DEFIANTLY tweeted MelDel now, and no one wrote
back for a while so Margaret decided she might as well make a
tape for a program where the winner gets to work for Donald
Trump. She knew she had no chance of winning, but she could be
a spitfire and say outrageous things, and sometimes that was more
important than winning.

When she had told Donny about her video audition idea, he
said, "Or you could apply for jobs."

"I will, I will," she said. They lived in a university town in Mississippi, and if you weren't a dental hygienist, like Donny, you had to work at the university. Which Margaret had, until a month ago.

It wasn't such a great job anyway, administrative assistant for an engineering professor. The professor was a woman, and she was always talking about her kids and how smart they were. When Margaret said, "You should go on *Wife Swap*," the woman looked alarmed and then asked Margaret to fax some documents to Austin. Margaret had lost her job because she spent too much time on her computer filling out applications for game shows, tweeting, checking to see if anyone had friended her, and trying to figure out who was ignoring her.

She was wondering if she should change her clothes for the video—it was eighty degrees, but she looked better in a turtleneck—when the doorbell rang. A college-aged girl in a pink sorority sweatshirt stood on the front steps smiling at her. She had a thick blonde ponytail and her teeth looked like she'd never needed a root canal. "Hiya," she drawled. "My name is Delores, and this is going to sound weird, but I'm on a scavenger hunt, and I'm wondering if you have a pair of red mittens I can borrow."

"Red mittens," said Margaret. She saw the girl giving the camera a curious glance. "I'm making a tape. Wait here."

She had to dig all the way in the back of the storage closet, behind Donny's old climbing boots and camouflage jacket, from when he used to hunt. There were no mittens in the Winter Clothes box, because it never got cold enough in central Mississippi for mittens. They were in the Stuff box, sent to her by her mother last Christmas with a note saying, *Just some of your little things I didn't have the heart to throw out. Cute!!* Enclosed were Margaret's third grade composition book, a photo of her dressed as a cat for Halloween, her ballet shoes, and a pair of tiny red mittens. She pulled a black turtleneck out of the Winter Clothes box, too, might as well.

"I hope they weren't supposed to be grown-up mittens," Margaret told Delores.

"These are perfect," she said, beaming. "Thank you so much. I really want to win this thing."

"Losing is no fun," Margaret agreed.

Donny came home smelling of mint and rubber gloves. "You're not gonna to leave me," he said to her, "because you love me too much." He smacked her ass. He was right, of course. If only he would just give in about the babies. She was thirty-eight years old.

"If you're not going to man up and get the job done, then I'll find someone who will," she told him. She had heard a wife say this on a talk show, and the husband had burst into tears and promised to man up.

But Donny held her chin in his hands and said, "It's your hormones talking. Give it another couple of years."

"But I can't help it! It's a biological imperative!" She sniffled.

"So is death," he said, and kissed her.

The next afternoon, Delores was back, but she didn't return the mittens. "It turns out," she said, "this scavenger hunt is kind of an ongoing thing. I didn't wake you, did I?"

Margaret had put a bathrobe over her bathing suit before answering the door. "No, of course not," she said. "I was just making a tape where I'm supposed to be at the beach." She had been standing on a yellow seat cushion, wondering if it would look like a surfboard from the right angle. There was a show called *Beach Hut* that filmed in Malibu, and all she had to do was prove she was fun in the sun.

The girl was wearing the same pink sweatshirt. Margaret noticed now that the letters were too faded to read, not that she knew anything about sororities anyway. "So, what I need now is a postcard from a European country. Would you happen to have one of those?" She arched her eyebrow at Margaret the way investigators did on TV when they were tricking the criminal into confessing.

"Right," said Margaret. "I wish."

Delores seemed pleased with this response for some reason. "Excellent!" she said. "A cork from a bottle of Spanish wine?"

"A can of Budweiser is more like it," Margaret said and then cleared her throat because she had already had two tallboys today, and it was barely four o'clock. She thought it might make her seem fun on her audition tape.

"Okay, well what about a white cupcake-shaped ceramic music box that says You're Very Special across it in pink script and plays 'Edelweiss.'"

Margaret felt her heart lurch a little. "Oh my," she said. "I have one of those."

It was in a box up in the crawl space. "I appreciate you going to all this trouble!" Delores called from below while Margaret pawed carefully through the pink fiberglass. Why oh why had she and Donny not gotten rid of all this junk? There was even a box of *National Geographic* magazines.

Margaret handed down a battered Thom McAn shoebox. "This is sort of where old Christmas presents go to die," she said, as she made her way down the ladder.

On the living room carpet, they pulled out the contents of the box—a Hallmark ornament of a cat on a Christmas tree, a pair of shiny fake-gold candlesticks, and the music box. "My mother gave this to me when I was way too old for it," Margaret said. "What thirty-year-old woman wants a music box?"

"It's pretty," said Delores, holding it as if it might break. Margaret thought of saying, "Just keep it!" but then what if her mother came to visit and wondered where it was? She was always threatening to visit. "This is some scavenger hunt," Margaret said.

"I worry that we're drifting apart," Margaret told Donny. "So drift more toward me."

"I'm not doing Facebook," he said. "And you need real friends."

She pretended not to hear him. "We could try out for a reality show together," she suggested, and when he didn't say anything she said, "I just want some of the finer things in life, that's all I want. We're not going to get them with good old-fashioned hard work, so why not be on TV?"

"What fine things do you want?"

"Trips to Europe. Spanish wine. I want dresses that come from a store that doesn't have the word *mart* in its name."

"This is all because you're mad about the babies," Donny said. "When we got married, you didn't want babies, and in another couple of years you'll come back to your senses. We just need to stick it out until then. We have fun together, just you and me."

"We go out for tacos on Fridays," she said, and he said, "See?"

She had no idea who it was babbling on the other end of the phone, but eventually she figured out it was the insect girl from the game show—or Amanda, as she was apparently called. "I was thinking about you," said Amanda. "I'm in town. Can you see me?"

They had exchanged phone numbers and fake hugs in the green room after the show, but Margaret hadn't expected they would actually keep in touch.

"I thought you lived all the way in Kansas City," she said.

"I do, but I'm staying at the Comfort Suites. I need to see you!" She sounded a little crazy. Margaret was almost finished recording a tape expressing her desire to live in a house full of ranting lunatics, serving as the "calm voice of reason, or if that's not fun enough, to encourage my housemates to do incredibly stupid things."

"Sure," she said to Amanda.

Amanda's hair was flatter and greasier than it was on the game show, but she looked just as happy as she had after solving the puzzle and winning twenty-five grand. "I had a fight with my boyfriend, but he's going to marry me because now I'm rich." She smiled; apparently, this didn't bother her. "But he said I had to get rid of some of my very prized possessions. And I thought of you! I don't know why, you were just nice. And I don't have a ton of friends."

Margaret sat on the edge of the king-sized bed and bounced a little in anticipation. "That's very kind of you," she said. "I'm sure I couldn't take anything valuable," she added, because of course she knew she could.

Amanda was standing next to a cloth-draped object beside the ice bucket, grinning like she had when the confetti fell from the ceiling at the TV studio. She pulled the cloth off to reveal what looked like a shoebox-sized clear plastic aquarium. Only instead of fish, there was dirt. And more dirt. And two oblong creatures moving around in the dirt.

"Good God," said Margaret. "I saw someone eat those on a reality show once." She was on her knees, staring.

"They're scarabs," Amanda said. "They're beautiful and sacred."

"Oh, they are!" cried Margaret. They seemed to glow, their brown bodies shining like jewels, their wings a glimmering, iridescent gold.

"There's some cow poo in there," Amanda said. "Just so you know."

"They're dung beetles," said Donny. "They spend their days rolling up balls of shit. But that's cool. At least they're keeping busy, being productive members of society." He gave her a look that suggested she could learn a thing or two from the dung beetles.

"They're scarabs," she said. "Egyptians worshipped them because they roll the sun across the sky."

"I can see that," said Donny.

She took a picture of the two beetles in their cage and posted them on Facebook. The reactions were immature: *Ick, Gross*, and the like. *They are beautiful and sacred!* she wrote. *Maybe you can't tell so much from the pix, but trust me.* Sometimes instead of making videos or tweeting, she would just stare at them as they rolled their big balls of dung. She liked to carry their cage from room to room with her. She read about them online and found herself hoping that they would lay eggs (or that at least one of them would) and that she would have a whole cage full of glimmering creatures and smooth round balls. Sometimes instead of going to bed, she would stay in the living room (Donny didn't want them in the bedroom) and put them on the top of the TV and stare at them. They had little faces, and she was almost sure the black glittering eyes were smiling at her.

One Friday afternoon, Donny said he needed to get away, clear his head. "To the cabin," he said, but there wasn't really a cabin, just a rundown shack out in the Alabama woods where his family used to stay during hunting season. "You could come with me," he offered, but they both knew she wouldn't. He had taken her there once, and when Donny said, "I can skin a squirrel, you want to watch?" she had threatened to leave. There was no cell phone reception or even dial-up out there. Not even dial-up! Before he left, Donny said, "Good luck with your audition tapes. I'll be back in a week." Then he sighed and left without kissing her good-bye.

"I know you're probably surprised to see me yet again," said Delores. "But I need something else, if you don't mind."

"What if I do mind?" Margaret said. "Just kidding." Although she really wasn't. She had asked some of her Facebook friends if they'd heard of any "on-going scavenger hunts" and several people—including her old boss, the engineering professor—wrote to tell her it was clearly a scam, and to expect to be robbed.

Delores frowned. "I need a stuffed white bunny wearing a homemade gingham apron. Also, a blue hot water bottle, and a soft white towel that was never used. Check the top of Donny's closet—his mother sent you those for Christmas and you forgot about them. Dig around while you're in there and grab me a gnome diary, but rip out the first three pages because you wrote in them when you were fourteen."

It wasn't as if Margaret *decided* to get these things, or even knew where to find them, but suddenly she was moving through the house, rooting through drawers and closets—the towel and the old diary right where Delores said they would be.

Please don't take the scarabs, she thought, as she handed everything over. Just not the scarabs. I love those damn bugs, she realized, and tried not to cry at how pathetic she was.

"And go ahead and email me those videos of yourself," Delores said, "while you're at it."

"Is this a robbery?" Margaret asked at last, when she'd hit Send and put the pile of objects at Delores' sandaled, red-toenailed feet.

"Does a robber give you presents?" Delores said, and produced a box from seemingly nowhere. "For your trouble," she said. "I shoplifted it for you." And she handed Margaret a pregnancy test.

Donny had gone out to the wilderness to get away from her, and now she couldn't even call to tell him the good news! Or was it good? It was news. At first she thought: *It's a miracle,* and then she realized that she'd been so obsessed with audition tapes and scarabs that she hadn't taken her pills in almost a month.

Before she left, Delores had asked for something to carry her things in.

"*My* things," Margaret corrected, tossing everything into a Wal-Mart bag. "I don't think this is a scavenger hunt at all!"

"These aren't for me," said Delores. "They're for my baby. The mittens and blanket and hot water bottle are to keep her warm when I take her to the north, the music box is so she'll know how much I love her, the bunny is to keep her laughing, and the diary is so she can get out her feelings on paper when she's going through those awkward teenaged years. The towel is just because everyone needs a towel. The videos are so if she ever finds out about you, I can show them to her and she can realize how much better off she is with me, because you're a lunatic. I'll come back tomorrow for that box of scrapbooking stuff you bought at Wal-Mart last year and never got around to using. I think I'll like to scrapbook." She smiled. "When she grows up, she's going to send me postcards from Europe and drink expensive Spanish wine, and marry a minor prince. You'll probably see her in fashion magazines."

"She'll have the finer things in life," Margaret said miserably. "But why do you want *my* baby?"

"Ask your mother if she remembers an old sorority sister named Delores who wanted to come to her baby shower and she said, 'No, you're just a dumb mooch,' and then I said, 'I curse your baby girl, and I will take her firstborn as my own.' Ask her if she remembers *that*."

"Oh, her," said Margaret's mother. "Delores was always eating our food and never replacing it. Did you see her? How does she look?"

"It turns out she's a never-aging sorority girl scavenger-fairy," Margaret said. "She looks good."

"Well, what on earth did she want?"

Margaret stared at the two pink lines on the pregnancy test. "Just to say hi," she said to her mother, who evidently didn't have the best memory in the world.

As a child, Margaret had held her parents' dinner guests hostage with her rendition of "The Good Ship Lollipop," because she had seen Cindy Brady do it. But otherwise, she had been content with her parents' attention, then her boyfriends', then Donny's. She hadn't realized she craved another, tinier audience until midway through her thirty-seventh year, when she woke up one morning sobbing and not knowing why. Only gradually as the day went on—the typing of memos, the answering of phone calls, the lonely lunch at her desk—did she understand what was wrong with her, what she wanted. *Is it unreasonable to want this?* she had tweeted, and pretty much everyone said she wasn't. *You go get what you want, gurl*, said someone called RacyLacy.

When Margaret had asked Delores, "How on earth did you even find me?" Delores laughed and said, "Credit check, Google, YouTube, Facebook, Twitter. I couldn't have not-found you if I'd tried."

Food, trees, shelter, water, fire. What more could a growing child need? It was worth a shot anyway.

She took the lid off the plastic cage and tipped it over, telling the scarabs, "The world is full of shit. Go and enjoy." Then she got in her car and headed up the street to refuel for possibly the very last time. Who needed a car in the wilderness? She wondered what would happen when Delores came back and found no one home—

the front door wide open and a note taped to it: *Take everything!* Maybe other scavengers would already be there, carting out the computer, video recorder, the big screen TV, the credit cards, the iPhones—staring bewildered at the open box of funny-smelling dirt on the floor. By then the scarabs would already be safely away, rolling, rolling, rolling the sun across the world while the humans filled their arms with all they could hold.

ARCTIC CIRCUS

1

By Thanksgiving, Amy had not said a word in eight days and was considering the possibility that she might never speak again. She lay on the sofa with her eyes closed and her hands clasped over her chest, like a vampire. Her grandmother and mother were in the kitchen, and her mother was saying, "Oh ho! That's cranberry sauce!" Talking to Booma as if she were a three-year-old. Something wet dripped on Amy's forehead, and she opened her eyes to see her older sister, Sheila, squeezing a grimy red dishrag over her. "Hey, loser," Sheila said loudly. "Wake up. I eloped." She peered down expectantly, as if this was the sort of news that would make Amy start talking again.

Amy stretched one foot off the couch, pointing her toes toward the wall. In the last week, Sheila had informed her that their mother was dead, the house was on fire, Booma had fallen out of her wheelchair ("Call 911, you idiot!"), and a bird was stuck in the garbage disposal. She had even held up the phone and threatened to dial the number of Jason Gerber, biggest geek in Amy's fifth grade class, and ask him out. "Hi, this is Amy," Sheila said in a breathless voice. "And I'm in love with you, you big sexpot." But Sheila didn't have the number and there were twenty Gerbers in the phone book, so there was nothing she could do.

Sheila made a disgusted, phlegmy noise in her throat and stomped back to the kitchen while Amy continued to lift her feet into the air, one at a time, pointing and flexing like she learned in ballet class. A moment later, Sheila and her boyfriend, Buddy, came thudding into the living room and Amy lowered her foot, closed her eyes. Buddy was the only boy Sheila had ever brought home, the only boy—not counting neighbor kids selling candy or magazines, not counting relatives—who had set ever foot in their house.

Buddy was not cute, and if Amy were talking she would tell him this. She would ask him if he was really a juvenile delinquent or just played one on TV. According to Sheila, they were having sex and lots of it. Amy frowned, trying to banish the image, picturing instead layers and layers of cartoon thought bubbles, popping open and dumping words out into the air like snow, covering Buddy and Sheila. Covering her mother. Covering Booma in her wheelchair. She could hear Sheila and Buddy behind her, crunching on something. Then somebody smacked the back of the sofa and they both went pounding up the steps.

In the kitchen, her mother was slamming pans around, humming something that sounded vaguely familiar, a TV theme song. Amy's mother hummed a lot, all the time it seemed; she hummed when she was watching TV, when she was fixing dinner, when she was in Booma's room, in the car. Once Sheila said, "Will you cut that out?" and her mother said, "Cut *what* out?" looking genuinely baffled.

The doorbell rang twice before Amy's mother stopped humming and shouted for somebody to please answer it. "Will you get that?" she screamed. "Somebody?" The bell rang again and as her mother huffed and stomped in the kitchen, Amy dragged herself to the front door to let her father inside. He was stooped over, trying to look in the dining room window, holding a prepackaged pie as if aiming to throw it. Amy pulled the door open and a rush of cold air jingled the copper wind chimes in the hall and whuffled the newspaper on the steps.

"Hey," her father said. "I'd hug you but I'd squash the pie."

Amy nodded. They already had pie, they had a million different kinds of pie, but he would find this out for himself. One thing she had figured out since she'd stopped talking: Most of the things people said were unnecessary, completely useless, things they would know on their own if they would just shut up long enough to think. She did a half turn on the tips of her toes and marched toward the kitchen. Her father was wearing his squeaky shoes, and the sound of them behind her made Amy feel mean.

"Squeak, squeak," her father said. "I'm here!" he called into the kitchen. He kissed Amy's mother on the cheek and then kissed the air around Booma's face, saying in a loud, fake-happy voice, "You sure look spiffy, Betty Sue!"

Booma's left eye quivered. She was wearing a turquoise turban and a lime-green velour housecoat. Her hands were lying on the arms of her wheelchair like things that didn't belong to her. Amy didn't look at Booma's face if she could help it. Sometimes it seemed as if she could see right through Booma's white, puddingy skin into her blood vessels and muscles and bones.

"She does look pretty," Amy's mother said. "I'll take that pie."

Amy glared at the top of Booma's turban. She pictured a worm in there, a little pink worm burrowing its way through Booma's brain as if it were an apple, turning it into mush.

"You could set the table, Amy," Amy's mother said.

The turban looked as if it were creeping in slow waves toward the top of Booma's forehead. Amy did not move. A brown cloth napkin swiped her across the cheek.

"Set it!" said her mother.

Amy scowled and grabbed a handful of forks from the cutlery drawer.

"Where's Sheila?" said her father, craning his head up and around as if he might find her crouched on the ceiling like a spider.

Amy clattered the forks on the kitchen table. *Upstairs having sex with Buddy*, said her thought bubble. She rolled her eyes, stuck her finger into her throat. Her father stared at her.

"What?" he said, and Amy realized that he did not know she wasn't speaking, that no one had thought to tell him.

"She's upstairs with her friend Buddy," said Amy's mother. "We're eating in the dining room," she said to Amy. "Please set the *dining* room table."

Booma was planted right in front of the doorway, her turquoise head lolling.

"Who's Buddy?" said Amy's father.

Amy squeezed past Booma's wheelchair as quickly as she could, but she still caught a whiff of her warm, sour-baby smell. Sour baby mixed with roses.

"Come in here and watch the parade with me, Betty Sue," said Amy's father in his cheery, fake voice, wheeling Booma out of the doorway. "Does anybody mind if I turn on the TV?"

Amy sniffed loudly and tossed the silverware on the dining room table with a satisfying clang. *You bought it*, she thought. *You do what you want.* But her father didn't do anything until her mother said, "Of course, turn it on." Granting permission, as if she were suddenly his mother, too.

"When are we expecting Emma?" her father called over the TV noise. Emma was the nurse who took care of Booma, who gave her injections and fed her what looked like baby food with a spoon. She was Booma's own age, maybe older, and she talked to Booma as if the two of them had been best friends all their lives: "How you doing today, Betty Sue? What say I paint your nails seashell pink?"

"She's not coming. Roy's getting back in town this afternoon so she's fixing dinner at their house."

Roy was Emma's husband. He was always going on business trips—something to do with cellular phones, Amy had gathered—and yesterday morning Amy had heard Emma telling her mother that he might not be back for Thanksgiving. "Well, come have dinner with us," her mother had said. Amy didn't know if she was disappointed or relieved that Emma wouldn't be there, or if she was simply jealous. Jealous of everybody who was not in her house with her family.

"No Emma?" Her father sounded worried, as if he was afraid Booma would suddenly drop dead right there at the table if Emma wasn't around to take care of her.

In the dining room, six orange placemats were already laid out in front of six chairs, and gourds spilled from a cornucopia like tiny shrunken heads. The curtains were open, and Amy could see Mr. Welsh across the street, stringing Christmas lights through his pine tree. Last year, Booma had asked if that was a Maryland tradition, putting Christmas lights up on Thanksgiving, and Amy told her it was just Mr. Welsh's tradition.

"Because we don't do that in Florida," Booma said. "But since I live here now I'm willing to adapt. You want to dig out the lights? Put up a tree?"

"I don't think so," Amy said. "Not yet."

"Open some presents?"

"You got presents?"

"Well, no," Booma said.

Booma had just moved into the guest room last year, but it wasn't a sick room yet, and it didn't smell funny—like old milk and rubbing alcohol. Booma still had all her hair, and she could get around just fine, and after Thanksgiving dinner the five of them had gone for a walk along the pier to the Concord Lighthouse. Sheila and Amy had gone up to the top together and waved at their parents and Booma below. Her father was still living with them, and there was no Emma, and Sheila didn't stay out till eleven o'clock every night. Now, whenever Amy's mother complained about never seeing her, Sheila said, "You don't expect me to stay around this hellhole, do you?"

Amy pictured the house as a tube of toothpaste, rolling itself up, squeezing all of them out of it. "Why don't you have friends over?" her mother used to say, but the last time she'd had a friend over they'd gone past the guest room and there was Emma changing Booma's diaper.

When Amy went back to the kitchen for napkins, the oven was open and the turkey was hissing inside it. "Here," Amy's mother said. "I'll finish that. Go get your sister."

Amy nodded and spun, tip-toed, in the direction of the hallway.

Her silence wasn't something Amy had planned, or even thought about before it happened. And it happened almost without her realizing it—on the bus home from school last week she realized, as she watched the dead, damp trees slide past her window, that she had not said a word all day. She hadn't spoken at breakfast—her mother had plopped an egg on her plate and then gone off to Booma's room. She hadn't been called on in class, she hadn't said hello to anyone and no one had said it to her. She felt strangely pure, hollowed out in a clean, beautiful way. Of course, · things had gotten slightly more complicated in the days since then—her teachers were starting to notice, and her classmates stared at her as if she were suddenly dying of some disease.

Sheila, astonishingly, had been the first to realize what was going on. "I wish you'd've stopped talking ages ago," she said. Then: "We'll see how long you can keep it up." Her mother, once she figured it out, said simply, "Oh, you're not talking? You can still listen though, right? So take the trash out, please." Now she didn't say anything about it, as if Amy had never spoken to begin with, as if everything were perfectly normal and fine. Last night Amy had tossed objects against her bedroom wall—shoes and books, her umbrella—until Sheila pounded on her door and said, "Shut the hell up." Their mother didn't come out of her room.

In the living room, Amy's father was sitting stiffly on the sofa, one leg flung over the other one, with a *National Geographic* balanced on his lap. Booma was on the other side of the room, staring at the giant Bart Simpson balloon bobbing over New York City. Amy went upstairs, but instead of knocking on Sheila's door (were bedsprings squeaking?) she went into her own room and shut the door. Beneath her feet, the whole house seemed to be vibrating gently, like something about to collapse or burst open. She lay down on her bed, closed her eyes, and waited.

2

Bedsprings were not squeaking in Sheila's room; in fact, Sheila and Buddy had climbed out her window and down the scrawny oak tree and were now making their way toward the 7-Eleven, where they would purchase Sun Chips and wine coolers. Buddy had a fake ID and he looked twenty-one anyway, with his goatee and his wrinkly eyes.

"Let's not go back," Sheila said. "Let's go to your house and stay there."

Buddy didn't say anything, but he dug his hand out of his pocket and grabbed hold of hers. She felt like a character in a movie, about to be whisked out of the path of a speeding car. She allowed herself to consider the possibility that he might be in love with her. "Do you ever feel like you're being chased?" she asked experimentally. "Or pretend you are or something?"

"I like to do the chasing," Buddy said, not looking at her, letting go of her hand. Of course he wasn't in love with her, she realized miserably. What was she thinking? And what did he mean—that he knew *she* was chasing *him* and wished she would stop? "We'll get drunk at my place," he said, "and then go back and eat turkey at yours."

"Okay," said Sheila, feeling wobbly with relief: he didn't hate her guts. She waited for him outside the 7-Eleven, propping herself up next to the pay phone. She dug a slightly bent Camel Light out of her jeans pocket and lit it, sheltering it with one hand, and imagined—as she sometimes did—herself being filmed by an invisible camera and her image magically projected onto a television screen that her mother could watch but do nothing about. Or sometimes her father was watching, or Amy, or Booma, depending on what she was doing and who would most disapprove.

When she and Buddy were climbing out her window, it was Booma watching her—Booma before she had brain cancer, when she would have squawked about how children should respect their parents and not go sneaking out of houses and so forth. When she would have gone tight-lipped and then quivery with helpless despair as her granddaughter—young and free and reckless!—went off to get drunk with a boy Booma would have called nasty. Sheila felt a surprising pang of regret when she considered that Booma would never meet any of her normal boyfriends, assuming she ever had any.

The sky seemed to be clearing. Puddles of blue appeared, the same blue as the mushroom-shaped water tower hovering above the trees. Sheila had been hoping it would rain again—it was drizzling this morning when she got up—and that Buddy would wrap his arms around her as they walked to his house. If it was raining hard enough, maybe they would stay there and not go back for turkey at all. Maybe he would kiss her like he did two nights ago, when they were stoned and walking on the pier around the bay. It was Amy watching then, shocked and jealous. Amy wishing she were there, too.

Maybe, Sheila thought, she and Buddy would do other things, if she was drunk enough, if she could get him drunk enough. She wanted something interesting to happen. She crushed her cigarette under her heel and lit another one.

Buddy was a senior, two years and one grade older than Sheila. She'd had a crush on him since the ninth grade, when she used to see him at the bus stop, standing off by himself, staring down the street at nothing. She watched him out of the corner of her eye, nodding while Geri Dundoor rattled on about the French test but hearing nothing, as if she had slid out of her body like a ghost and was standing invisible next to Buddy, whispering in his ear.

Whispering *You are beautiful. Look at me.*

And the strange thing was, she *didn't* think he was beautiful at all. He was shorter than she preferred, and his hair was both too poofy and too greasy at the same time. He looked dirty and he looked mean, and she loved him. It was almost a relief when he stopped taking the bus. Sometimes she'd see him slamming in or out of a rusty gold car in the school parking lot.

And then two weeks ago she'd overslept, and instead of running to catch the bus (she imagined her backpack flapping against her shoulders, her scarf floating behind her like a banner proclaiming her idiocy), she watched it pull away, far down the street. She stopped on the pavement and stood there. Her mother had already left for work, so Sheila would have to stay home from school. Or take a taxi, an idea that mortified her. She thought of going back to the house, telling Emma she suddenly wasn't feeling well—as if it mattered to Emma what Sheila did. She just sat in Booma's room all day reading *National Geographic* and *Sierra*, staring at pictures of deserts and volcanoes. Sheila had made up her mind to go home and sneak in the basement when she heard a roar and a radio—Van Halen, urging her to Jump!—and then Buddy was there telling her he'd give her a lift.

"Great," Sheila said, and suddenly she felt like somebody else, as if this were a play and she had been given certain lines, a certain role, a character that was not exactly hers but could be, if she worked hard enough at it. She got in Buddy's car and tossed her backpack into the backseat as if this was something she did every day. His car smelled mysteriously like sausages.

After that she made it a point to miss the bus.

Sheila understood in some small, dark part of herself that she and Buddy weren't actually dating—his kiss was too sloppy to be taken seriously, and sometimes she got the distinct feeling he found her annoying. Just yesterday, after he'd picked her up for school (he came to her house now and honked) he said, "I feel like a fucking chauffeur service." But he said it grinning, so she couldn't tell if he meant it. She usually took the school bus home.

One encouraging thing was that Buddy didn't seem to have any other girlfriends, and when Sheila told her friends about him they reacted with a general snort. "Scuzzy," was the word they used. Sheila found this thrilling. Buddy had a small group of pot-smoking, denim-jacket-wearing friends she sometimes saw him with; she wasn't interested in meeting any of them and Buddy wasn't interested in introducing her. Sometimes it seemed to Sheila as if it was enough just to be buoyed on the waves of her feelings, even if nothing ever happened, because nothing was *going* to happen. Then he'd do something like grab her hand, or kiss her, and she wouldn't be so sure anymore.

"I got Doritos instead," he said, striding over with a paper bag. "And a six-pack of Bud."

Sheila blushed. It had been her idea to get the wine coolers. She'd thought it seemed romantic, those berry flavors.

"Let's rock and roll," Buddy said, and he took off across the parking lot in his fast, bouncing walk, his thin shoulders looking sweet and fragile. She was going to seduce him—today, at his house, in his bed. Or maybe even in his living room, on the floor. She was going to lose her virginity to a scuzzy, pot-smoking boy who might not even like her. This thought touched her; she felt suddenly sorry for herself.

Last week she'd said to Amy, "Oh hey, I'm screwing this much older druggie guy. Don't tell anybody!" Then she'd laughed and said, "Guess I don't have to worry about that. I wish you'd've stopped talking ages ago." Today she'd almost told her sister, "Wake up, I'm pregnant," but couldn't bring herself to say it, as if that might doom her to its coming true.

Buddy lived three blocks from her house, so they headed back the way they'd come from. "Can I have a light?" Sheila said, just to get him to slow down and talk to her. "I want to be sure I'm smoking like a fiend when we walk past my house."

"We don't have to go past your house." He handed her his purple Bic lighter. "We just go up Prindle."

"I want to." She smiled in a way she hoped looked mischievous and sexy. Buddy shrugged and shifted the bag to his other arm, and too late Sheila realized how childish it was, prancing past her house hoping someone would see her. Hoping—she knew suddenly—that *Amy* would see her, Amy who couldn't say a word, could only watch her and wonder how she had changed into this person she didn't even know.

But no one was watching; no one was looking for her. The curtains in the living room were drawn, and if it wasn't for the two cars in the driveway it would look like nobody was home. Across the street, floating on the smell of pumpkin pie, Christmas music and loud voices were coming from Mr. Welsh's house. Mr. Welsh lived alone, but there were always cars parked in his driveway. There was always something going on at Mr. Welsh's.

"Should've gone up Prindle," Buddy said flatly.

It had been a horrible idea to invite him to Thanksgiving dinner, as if he even cared about meeting her stupid family. But when he'd told her his mother was going to Delaware with her boyfriend, she'd said, "Why don't you come to my house? Free turkey." And there was a long, thunderous, devastating silence until he said, "Yeah? Cool."

She had never been inside his house; she had never seen his mother. When he opened his front door—it was unlocked—she was disappointed to see how clean his living room was, cleaner even than her own. A dried floral arrangement sat primly in the middle of the coffee table. There was the faint odor of burnt cheese. She followed him into the kitchen and sat at his coupon-cluttered kitchen table. "I need a beer," she said. "I am so relieved to be out of that nuthouse. They're all insane."

"They don't seem *insane*," Buddy said, handing her a beer. She waited for him to sit down but he stayed where he was, leaning against the sink.

She had told him about her grandmother moving in and her father moving out, and Emma moving in—or practically, she was always there—and her mother being a bitch all the time and her sister not talking. Now she said, "You don't know what goes on. My room's right above my grandmother's?"

"What's that thing you call her?" Buddy interrupted suddenly. "Boomer?"

"Jesus," Sheila said. "Booma. When Amy was little she couldn't say 'grandma' so she called her Booma. And now my idiot mother still calls her that sometimes when she's talking to us." It had actually been Sheila who couldn't pronounce her name, but she wasn't about to tell Buddy this. Her grandmother had been hurt when, several years ago, Sheila refused to call her Booma anymore. "Anybody can be *grandmother*. Grandmother, grandma, blah blah blah. I liked having my own name. Amy'll still call me Booma, won't you, Amy?"

"Yes," said Amy. "I'll keep calling you that the rest of my life."

"Good for you," Sheila muttered, and was pleased to see her grandmother slit her eyes. It was something she used just because she could—this power to upset her grandmother, to evoke something so huge and terrible it could sweep them both away. Once Sheila started there was no stopping her. There was no stopping until her grandmother was crying and Sheila was banished to her room, shaking and weak.

Soon after her grandmother moved in, Sheila said, "So which of your stuff are you going to leave me when you croak?" waiting for the snap that would set them loose, whirling them both into that familiar, exhausting ritual. But her grandmother just said, "You and Amy can work that out, honey." The air felt soggy with illness. When her father moved out, Sheila begged him to take her with him, but he said, "This is where you're supposed to be right now," as if he knew anything at all about her. Her mother just let him go, didn't even try to talk him out of it. Sheila made it a point to stay away as much as possible, hanging out with her friends at the mall or McDonald's, sometimes going to a movie by herself. She did her homework late at night, drinking coffee from the 7-Eleven, eating Tootsie Rolls. Sometimes, lately, she could hear something happening downstairs; she'd open her vent, lie on the floor, and listen.

"My room's right above my grandma's," she repeated, surprised at the urgency in her voice.

"Grandma Boomer," Buddy said, nodding. "Go on."

"And sometimes at night I can hear my mother in there talking weird—like in some other language." She took a breath. She'd never told anyone about this and wasn't sure how to describe it, or if she should even be trying to. "It's like gibberish—but it goes on and on and on, and my grandmother does it, too, but she's sort of *croaking*. It's the weirdest thing I've ever heard in my life. It gives me the creeps."

"That's fucked up," Buddy said. "Maybe they're speaking French."

"They are *not* speaking French," Sheila said, irritated. She wished she hadn't told him. The whole thing seemed shameful for some reason, something she wasn't supposed to know about and should never mention.

"What's it sound like?" Buddy said. "I want to know what it sounds like." He pulled out a chair and sat down on it backward.

"I told you," she said. "It sounds like another language, like some weird language I've never heard before."

"I want to hear it. I want to come to your house and hear it. When we get over there I'm gonna ask your mom to do it."

"Don't *even*," Sheila cried, and was distressed to see Buddy flinch. "Please don't. It would just be embarrassing."

Buddy stared at her, tapped his finger on the table. His fingernail was flat and clean. Staring at it, Sheila was aware of paralysis traveling through her body like a heavy, damp vine. She was aware of ruining everything without trying to, without even knowing what was being ruined. She wondered then if her family had started eating dinner yet, without her. Her mother would insist they say the blessing, and everyone would clamp on to the hand of the person next to them. She thought of the two empty places where she and Buddy should be, and the missed opportunity to hold his hand, then begin the ritual of passing and scooping, lifting the plates around the table, knowing—for just the briefest amount of time—exactly where she was, and what would happen next.

3

When JoAnn informed Wayne that Sheila and Buddy were gone and that Amy was hiding out in her room, his first thought was that they were punishing him, everyone in cahoots to make him feel like shit.

"Should I leave?" he said. "Will that make everybody happy?"

"No," said JoAnn. "It would make *me* happy if everyone would eat together like a family."

"That," said Wayne, "isn't seeming too likely."

"No, it isn't," JoAnn agreed. The calmness of her voice irritated him. She stood in the doorway between the dining room and the kitchen, staring at him as if trying to make out where she'd seen him before. "Are you sure this is okay?" he'd asked her, over and over, when he decided to get an apartment. "Just for a while, to make things easier on everybody."

"Oh absolutely," she'd said.

"Just think of it as me going to a nursing home instead of her," Wayne said, trying to be funny. JoAnn just looked at him—the way she'd looked at him now—with a vague, puzzled expression. Then she'd gone down the hall to Betty Sue's room and shut the door.

Now she said, "You get Mom, and I'll finish putting things on the table."

Betty Sue was still in front of the television, her pale little head nodding gently with the parade music. She looked like an ancient queen sitting there, in her turban. She sighed.

"Oh, Betty Sue," Wayne said. "I miss you."

She looked at him sadly, he thought, as if she missed him, too.

"Are you ready for some turkey?" he said, steering her toward the dining room. He'd always hated it when people talked to the elderly as if they were retarded children, but here he was doing it himself.

"You-all had better put me in a nursing home when I start to get real bad," Betty Sue had told them. "Just put me in there with all the other hardly-ables."

"Hardly-ables?" Wayne asked.

"Hardly able to walk, hardly able to see, hardly able to hear." She laughed. She had been a nurse; she knew exactly what was happening to her.

But JoAnn decided not to put her in a nursing home, and it seemed to Wayne that if anyone should go anywhere it should be him. He told JoAnn it was so she could have more time with her mother, without having to worry about him.

"I don't worry about you," she said.

"You know. So you can have privacy."

She didn't say anything. Then: "I don't want to watch her die, either, Wayne." But she'd agreed, she'd said that maybe it would be better, just for a while. Wayne told himself he was doing it for them. He tried not to let himself believe that he intended to stay away until Betty Sue died. The last parent either of them had.

Twenty-four years ago, before he even knew her, JoAnn had come to his father's funeral. He recognized her from geography class—the shy, ruddy-faced girl who'd done the presentation on Nepal—but he couldn't remember her name. After the service she and Betty Sue sought out Wayne and his mother, Donna, and said how sorry they were and offered to do anything they could to help. "I have your homework assignments," JoAnn said and blushed a deeper red. "Not with me, I mean. I thought since you'd be staying home from school a few days." She was staring so intently at her shoes that her eyes looked almost closed. "When my dad died I didn't feel like going to school for a while."

Later, they would marvel at how something so tragic could have brought them together, how death had provided them with this gift. Their mothers never became fast friends, though they liked each other in a distantly affectionate way. His mother was a former charm school teacher who seemed always to be forcing her face into expressions it didn't want to assume—smiling when Wayne could tell she was annoyed, furrowing so she wouldn't laugh instead. After she'd died, Wayne discovered a blue spiral notebook in her bureau, full of entries detailing the chest pains she didn't want to bother anyone with.

The second time Betty Sue met Wayne and Donna, she told them about forgetting to take the baby bottle nipples out of the boiling water her first day at the hospital. "I ran down the hallway screaming, 'My nipples are burning! My nipples are burning!'" She laughed so hard she could hardly breathe. "Hoo whee. I made quite an impression, let me tell you."

"Oh, I'm sure," said Donna, twittering politely.

Wayne wheeled Betty Sue into the dining room and placed her next to JoAnn's chair. He was careful to avoid his old place at the head of the table, but too late he realized he was sitting across from the two of them. Two against one. The whole room felt unbalanced, the whole house—about to tilt him right out of it.

"You know what?" he said. "We should call Emma."

JoAnn looked at him.

"I'm calling her." He stood up and went into the kitchen. "Where's her number? Didn't it used to be on the fridge?"

"Why do you want to call Emma?"

"To wish her a happy Thanksgiving, of course! Oh, here it is." He was aware of a feeling of desperation as he dialed, as if he were calling the police or poison control. When Emma answered he said in a voice he hardly recognized, "Hiya, Emma! Wayne here."

"Oh, hello Wayne!" She sounded surprised, but not unpleasantly so. "Well, how are you today? Are you having a nice Thanksgiving?"

"I am," he said. "I was just calling to make sure Roy was still coming in today. Wouldn't want you to be all alone on Thanksgiving."

"He's here," Emma told him. "I've got him in the kitchen making the stuffing." She giggled, as if she'd made a joke.

"Well," said Wayne. From the dining room, he could hear JoAnn murmuring softly to her mother, the way their children used to talk to their stuffed animals. "I guess that's all."

"Thanks for calling," Emma said, sounding slightly bewildered.

Wayne kept listening for a moment after she'd hung up. Then he went back to the dining room and announced, "She's fine. Roy's there." He sat down. JoAnn was tucking a thick orange napkin into the neck of Betty Sue's robe, like a bib. "Would you like me to go get Amy?"

JoAnn shook her head, smoothed the napkin beneath her mother's chin. "She knows we're eating. Shall we say the blessing?" She reached out her hands. This was a tradition she had brought to their marriage, holding hands for the blessing.

He held JoAnn's cool hand and Betty Sue's warm limp one and bowed his head while JoAnn said, "Thank you for this food, this family. Thank you for taking care of us, amen."

"Amen," said Betty Sue, suddenly reviving. Her voice was flat and surprisingly loud. She nodded at Wayne and he smiled. She looked away. "Amen," she repeated, and JoAnn—who had not let go of her mother's hand after the blessing—leaned over and kissed it.

"The green bean casserole looks fantastic," said Wayne and was distressed when JoAnn suddenly stood up and went into the kitchen. Had he said something wrong? Was there anything he could say that wasn't wrong? But JoAnn reappeared with potholders and put them down in the middle of the table.

"Everything's hot," she said. "Don't want to burn your hands. Go on and start," she said, somewhat impatiently Wayne thought. To her mother she said: "Doesn't it look good?"

"Hmmm," said Betty Sue, who watched while JoAnn scooped stuffing on her plate.

When Betty Sue first moved in, the house had felt deceptively festive, the way it did when she came for Christmas or Easter or summer vacation. She would tell stories at the dinner table. Not about JoAnn's childhood hijinks but about her own childhood in Tennessee. About her little brother, Henry, who'd drowned when he was four. About meeting her husband, Nathan, at the boarding house her parents owned. "I was eighteen and he was thirty-seven, and neither of us thought anything of it."

"This is interesting. You should write all this down," Wayne said once, and Betty Sue gave him a dark look.

"I know I've got plenty of free time and all," she said, "but that doesn't mean I want to write my memoirs." She pronounced it *mem-wahs*, disdainfully.

Sometimes he told himself that if Betty Sue understood how things were now, she would forgive him. She would say it was all right for him to leave, just for a while, since there was nothing he could do anyway. Then he thought of her angry—the way she'd been when she'd found out he quit his job to go back to school without telling JoAnn about it first. "What kind of marriage is that?" she'd shrieked at him on the phone. "You just up and do what you want without taking your family into consideration? What the hell is that about?"

Of course it had worked out—his consulting job paid more than the advertising agency ever had—but she didn't forgive him right away, even after JoAnn had.

"How can you do such a crappy thing to JoAnn?" he could imagine her saying now. "You just up and do what you want?"

And there were times, late at night, when he thought: I'm ready to go back. I'll move back home tomorrow. But in the morning he knew he wouldn't, not quite yet.

JoAnn was cutting up food on Betty Sue's plate, slicing the turkey into tiny squares, pulling the bread apart and buttering it, the way she'd done for the children when they were young. Last Thanksgiving, Sheila had dropped her crescent roll on the floor and then leapt from her chair and jumped on it. "Don't stop me," she cried. "I'm on a roll!" Then she collapsed in her chair, hooting with laughter. Amy's iced tea had come out her nose, and Betty Sue had shaken her head and said, "You all," as if she couldn't figure them out. Wayne was just about to say something about how he wished the girls were here when Betty Sue croaked suddenly: "Scratch my head."

JoAnn carefully pulled off the turquoise turban and ran her fingers up and down Betty Sue's pale baby fuzz, over her pink scalp. "Up up up," said Betty Sue. "Ahh."

"Better?" said JoAnn.

Betty Sue nodded, her eyes half closed. Wayne could hear a car moving slowly down the street, and he wished he was in it, going somewhere, away from here.

"Too bad Amy and Sheila are otherwise occupied," he said. "They don't know what they're missing."

"There'll be leftovers," said JoAnn. She spooned some mashed potatoes into Betty Sue's mouth. "That's right," she said. "I used your recipe, Mom. With the bacon. How 'bout some beans?" Her own plate was empty.

Wayne felt a splinter of annoyance at being so obviously and intentionally ignored, then ashamed at his own selfishness. He should be grateful JoAnn invited him here at all. He filled his plate and then—"You're eating so fast, Wayne," said JoAnn— made a show of scraping it clean. He leaned back in his chair with a satisfied groan. "I'm going to burst in a minute," he said. "That was fantastic, JoAnn. Thanks for having me over. It's real important to me."

"It's important to me, too," JoAnn said, not looking at him.

"I don't even think I have room for pie," he said.

"You don't have to stay for pie."

"It's not that I don't want to stay, it's just that I don't really have room. Can I help you clean up?"

"We're not quite finished here, Wayne." Her voice was pleasant and detached, a voice he'd heard her use to ask strangers for directions. "Why don't you say good-bye to Amy before you leave?"

He deposited his dishes in the sink, rinsed them off, and put them in the dishwasher. The dishwasher was new—JoAnn had bought it since he'd moved out, something that made him feel uncomfortable, almost sad. Why not put in a dishwasher when he could enjoy it, too? It occurred to him—as he climbed the blue carpeted stairs, past the photos that marched chronologically up the wall—that he might never get to use that dishwasher. His apartment didn't have one, either.

There was no answer when he knocked on Amy's door, so he turned the knob and went in. She was lying on her bed, staring at him in a strange, unfocused way that made it seem as if she was looking right through him, into the hallway.

"I'm off!" Wayne said brightly. "Gotta hit the road."

Amy frowned and cleared her throat, crossed her arms over her chest.

"All right then," he said. "There's some fantastic turkey downstairs."

Amy rolled over on her stomach and waved the back of her hand at him, shooing him away. "Right," he said. "Is your sister in her room?" Amy didn't appear to hear him.

He was ashamed at how badly he wanted to get away, ashamed of the relief he felt when he pushed open Sheila's door and found no one there. Downstairs, he retrieved his coat from the living room. He kissed JoAnn on the cheek. He kissed Betty Sue on her papery forehead. "Bye for now," he said and felt a terrible love, a terrible pain. It followed him out the door, it followed him in his car to the end of the street, and it followed him around the corner to the Rite Aid, where he purchased Pepto-Bismol and a newspaper. It followed him all the way to his building, up the stairs, and into his yellow apartment—the place he had started, until just now, to think of as safe.

4

With Wayne gone and her mother tucked into bed, JoAnn cleared the table, brought the dishes—most of them still untouched, including her own—into the kitchen and stacked them next to the sink. Out the window, the backyard was damp and yellow, rolling out under a bruised sky. The Tuff Shed sat squatly on the place where the swing set had stood, years and years ago.

Over the past few months, JoAnn had begun fixing up the house—installed a dishwasher, wallpapered the master bedroom—and she'd thought it was just about keeping herself busy and distracted. But now it dawned on her that she was preparing to sell the house, to move away. She could rent a place in another part of town, an apartment maybe, or a townhouse. Close enough that the children could go to their same schools and she could keep her administrative assistant job—though lately she'd been looking through the classifieds, wondering if she could be something else. A travel agent. A dog groomer. She knew, though no one had said it, that her marriage was over. Even if Wayne wanted to come back, she wouldn't let him. If the house was sold, they could each take their share and start fresh.

She wrapped the turkey in tinfoil and packed the cranberry sauce, potatoes, and stuffing into Tupperware. Last year her mother had been horrified when she'd dumped the remaining tablespoon of gravy down the sink. "That's perfectly good!" she cried. "I'd've eaten that for lunch." She had been living with them only a month, and the tension between them coiled and stretched and slackened several times a day. She would be telling JoAnn that her house was a breeding ground for bacteria and then, suddenly, she'd tremble and smile and wrap JoAnn in her tight little arms. They would talk sometimes until midnight—sitting at the kitchen table, reminding each other of places and conversations, of the flowers in their Florida backyard, of neighbors long dead—and then the next morning her mother would complain bitterly that there weren't any apples in the house, or oatmeal, or sausage. She would pout and sit in her room. She said she was bored all day, watching television.

"What do you want me to do?" JoAnn said. "I have to go to work. Wayne has to go to work. The girls have to go to school. I'll be home at the usual time to take you to your doctor appointment."

"Leave me the car."

"Firstly, I need the car, and secondly, you can't be driving."

"Well goddammit," she said. "I feel like a zoo animal waiting to be put to sleep."

Then later she would apologize, crying, saying she was just scared and frustrated—"flusterated," she pronounced it—and tell JoAnn to please just put her in a home with the other hardly-ables. JoAnn ignored her until she calmed down.

In the weeks just after JoAnn's father died—with no warning at all, in a car accident on the way to Woolworth's to buy weed killer—her mother had been this same way. Crying one minute, cursing the next, always recovering and collapsing and recovering again. Then suddenly it was over; she gave away his clothes, his engineering books, his shoes. She packed him into boxes and donated him to the Goodwill store. "We don't need his suits to remember him," she'd said to JoAnn, who *did* need his suits, and his shoes, and his Brut-smelling shirts, and bought some of them back from Goodwill. His shoes for a dollar, shirts for fifty cents. She hid them in her closet in a garbage bag. What ever became of them? she wondered now, putting foil over the turkey. Had her mother found them and gotten rid of them once and for all? When they'd sold the house in Florida, JoAnn had everything shipped here. She rented a storage unit downtown and filled it with her mother's sewing machine and dusty blue sofa, her own high school papers and books. It was possible that the garbage bag was in there somewhere, stuffed between the boxes.

When she'd sealed up the last container of food, JoAnn realized she'd neglected her hostess duties by forgetting to wrap up a plate for Wayne, or giving him his pie to take back to his apartment. She'd never seen where he lived; he'd never invited her. The girls said his apartment was small and the walls were all yellow. Like pee? she wondered. Or like daffodils? Their first apartment had had a yellow kitchen, the walls so lemony you wanted to lick them. "In our first actual house," JoAnn had said, "let's paint each room a different color. Like, the Blue Room and the Green Room."

"The Chartreuse Room," said Wayne. "For people we want to leave soon."

"The Puke-Brown Room for Jehovah's Witnesses!" said JoAnn. They had more than twenty different rooms in their first, imaginary house, a crayon box full.

How many futures were there to mourn? The one with her husband; the one with her mother—who was only sixty-eight, who should not be dying yet; the one with her daughters bringing their husbands and children back to this house, sleeping in their old beds. All her losses seemed to flow into each other, until she couldn't tell which was which.

Upstairs, a door opened and shut, a toilet flushed. Amy. Amy, JoAnn had decided, would be just fine, would be more fine than of any of them. When her teacher called to ask if anything was wrong—why wasn't Amy talking?—JoAnn felt resentment on behalf of her daughter. "If she doesn't want to talk," she said to squeaky little Ms. Grable, "why should she talk? What's the big deal?"

"Well," said Ms. Grable doubtfully. "I *will* have to mark off for class participation." Then she suggested Amy might want to talk to the guidance counselor, and JoAnn suggested she concern herself with the children who had actual problems, parents on crack or no shoes to wear.

Sheila was the one JoAnn worried about. Sheila who disappeared for hours at night and showed up with strange-looking boys. When JoAnn once attempted to talk to her about drugs and sex, Sheila had shrieked, "Fuck you!" and slammed out the back door. Now, whenever JoAnn got too near, Sheila flinched as if she'd been struck. Sheila was the one who would run away, or end up pregnant, or have a car accident. Which was another reason for moving, JoAnn told herself, irrationally—as if the house itself were giving off some toxic substance infecting her oldest daughter.

When the dishes were cleared and cleaned, all traces of holiday spirit packed up and put away, JoAnn went into her mother's room. She was sleeping with her head turned slightly to the side, as if listening to some voice whispering from the depths of her pillow. There was a travel magazine lying open on Emma's chair and JoAnn moved it to the floor, careful not to lose her place.

Two days ago, JoAnn had picked up one of Emma's magazines and started reading an article called "The Arctic Circus" about the fun adventures you can have at the North Pole, if you want to spend thousands of dollars and risk your life a little bit. The most interesting part of the article was about a group of Canadians and Americans who'd made a fantastically expensive and treacherous journey to the North Pole on icebreaker ships, only to arrive and see a group of costumed Russian children dancing and singing. A helicopter hovered overhead, filming them for a Russian television program. JoAnn had laughed out loud when she read that. "Can you imagine the look on their faces?" she'd said to her sleeping mother. "The children weren't even wearing coats."

Now there was a new magazine, featuring scuba diving in Belize. Emma was saving for a trip next summer, to Kenya or India, Australia or the North Pole. She hadn't decided yet. "I've never been west of the Mississippi," she told JoAnn once, almost proudly. "So if I'm going somewhere, I'm going somewhere big." She was going with her husband, Roy. Roy dropped Emma off every morning and picked her up every evening in his red truck.

JoAnn liked to think that if her mother had met Emma under different circumstances, they would be friends. Maybe her mother would want to go to Belize or Australia. She had never been west of the Mississippi, either.

JoAnn picked up her mother's hand and held it, a naked little bird. "Mama," she said quietly. "Mommy. Mother. Momma. Mom." Sometimes her mother talked in her sleep, not using any words JoAnn recognized. And then JoAnn would talk, too—or rather, she would babble along with her—as if they were two infants speaking their own language of want. There were times when her mother chattered so loudly and with such urgency that JoAnn felt as helpless as when Sheila was a baby, demanding something of her, furious that JoAnn couldn't provide it or even understand what she needed. Instead, JoAnn would hold Sheila in her lap and rock her back and forth, murmuring comforting, senseless words, sounds that meant nothing but somehow quieted Sheila down, lulled her into sleep.

"You're going to screw up her entire language system," Wayne had warned her. "Babies need to absorb syntax."

"She has plenty of time to absorb syntax," said JoAnn. "But first she has to stop crying, which is what I'm trying to get her to do."

Wayne had insisted they use flashcards, which Sheila liked to chew on and, when she was older, fling across the room like twirly leaves. The flashcards would balance out JoAnn's baby talk, he told her; and maybe he was right. Maybe Sheila would be learning disabled if he hadn't done his part. And maybe she would be a sixteen-year-old college graduate if JoAnn had spoken to her only in complete sentences, infusing her baby brain with the correct usage of gerunds and prepositional phrases.

Had Amy demanded less? Or had JoAnn just known more easily what she wanted? Amy was the calm baby, the baby who watched, who stared at her flashcards for long minutes before chewing them up. Even Amy's crying had seemed calm, more like an announcement than a plea. That was the way her silence seemed now—not a cry for help, as Ms. Grable would like to believe, but a simple statement of fact: I don't have anything to say to you.

JoAnn heard Amy creak down the stairs, go into the kitchen, and open the refrigerator. Then Sheila—opening the front door, slamming it shut, sighing heavily. One set of footsteps, no Buddy this time. JoAnn located her family in her mind: Sheila in the foyer, and Amy in the kitchen. She pictured Wayne in a dim room with yellow walls—like daffodils, she decided—watching television alone. Everyone stranded, like her mother, someplace out of JoAnn's reach.

She knew she could have put her mother in a nursing home and kept her family intact. They had even gone to look at a place—she and Wayne and her mother. It was only fifteen miles away, right on JoAnn's way to work. "Looks good to me," her mother had said. "Sign me up!"

But they hadn't signed her up. That night, as she and Wayne were looking through the insurance papers, she decided they were not *going* to sign her up. "She's staying here," JoAnn told him, and he looked at her as if she'd done something unspeakably horrible, injected an incurable virus right into their family's heart. Which, she knew, is exactly what she did.

Her mother had protested bitterly. "If you don't put me in that home, I'll never forgive you." She looked stern, then tearful. "Why do you want to do this to yourself?"

"I'm not doing anything to anybody," said JoAnn.

Now, alone in the quiet with her mother, she could hear Sheila making her way down the hall to the kitchen. JoAnn held her breath while she waited—for what? For something to happen, but she couldn't say what it was. For her children to sit at the table, eating Thanksgiving dinner together, she supposed. For her mother to wake up and ask for some pie. For Wayne to have never left them. For everyone to be happy and celebrating. The microwave beeped. There was the clatter of plates and glasses, the running of tap water, then a trample of feet, as if her daughters were moving in circles around one another.

Puppet Town

Once there was a town where everyone wore a puppet on their right hand, as decreed by law, moral code, and common sense. Many years earlier (before anyone could remember) a man came through town wearing a burlap sack on his right hand, with two buttons sewn on for eyes. There were paintings in the town's historical society depicting the man thrusting out his sacked hand as if to hold back the wind, the townspeople on their knees before it.

A local woman recorded the events in her diary, also on display in the historical society. "I am pure," shouted the puppet, in a high and reedy voice, "and because I am pure, so is he." He gestured at the man. "We live honestly and humbly." Then the puppet dipped into a giant wooden box and reappeared with tiny burlap sacks clutched in his burlap mouth. He tossed them into the crowd, and the townspeople cheered.

Before the puppet-prophet came to town, there had been much sin and licentiousness, gambling and fornicating. But with the coming of the puppets, everything changed. At the craps tables, the puppets refused to play, spitting the dice across the room. Even the left-handed gamblers quailed before the watchful button eyes, eventually putting on their hats and going home. The saloon closed down within three months and reopened as a burlap and button store. The prostitutes grew sore from the rough burlap spankings; their customers grew tired of the puppets' high chattering voices preaching against sin. When the puppets went on this way, it was impossible to interrupt them.

Wives were pleased to learn that the puppets were excellent cooks and helpmates. A wife's puppet was always ready to assist her with a hot pan, offer recipe advice, or push the mop. Sometimes a husband would come home from work and find his wife sitting at the kitchen table, laughing at something her puppet was saying. When a man and his wife were alone in the bedroom, their puppets would ask politely to be placed in a bureau drawer.

Years passed, and the town became more isolated as fewer and fewer of its citizens ventured beyond it. The puppets encouraged this, cautioning the humans about the dangers of a world where both hands were naked to perform unmentionable acts of depravity. (The puppets would refuse to mention these acts, shaking their heads and rattling their eyes.) The puppets were made of blue felt now, rather than burlap, and their eyes resembled human eyes, and their mouths were wide and red. Some of them had teeth.

More and more, husbands and wives would retreat to their bedrooms and find that their puppets wanted to talk about politics and puppet rights rather than go silently into the bureau. When the birth rate began to drop, the puppets ordered the husbands and wives to sleep together, even though the puppets hovered above and around them, and sometimes (it was whispered) asked to take part.

Every once in a while, a young man and a young woman would sneak off to the forest outside of town and remove their puppets and stare into each other's eyes, four naked hands fumbling, and speak to each other in their real voices. Many of them had forgotten what their real voices sounded like. Sometimes they fell in love, but usually they left the forest feeling annoyed and ashamed, their puppets tsk-tsking at them as they drove home.

And sometimes a teenager would rip the puppet off and throw it on the ground, vowing never to listen to it again, only to realize hours or minutes later that they had no idea how to live without that small, high voice and those stern plastic eyes. "I'm sorry," they would murmur, stroking the blue felt. "Please forgive me."

The puppets usually did, but not always.

And so, as time went on, a kind truck driver on the El Paso to San Francisco route knew to expect hitchhikers on the highway outside of Puppet Town: all teenagers—boys and girls— all with the same look of terror on their faces, their right hands shoved into jacket pockets. Sometimes they wept softly, and the truck driver offered them Kleenex but didn't pry. They spoke in whispers. When they thought he wasn't looking, he would catch them staring at their pale right hands, their mouths slack with fear or wonder, moving their fingers as if pushing invisible buttons.

Sometimes they left him at the first pit stop, and sometimes they made it all the way to his destination. It was always a relief to leave them, to honk his horn and wish them well. The only time they seemed perfectly normal—like himself at sixteen, far from home and ready for adventure—was when they were in his rearview mirror, waving good-bye.

Good Listener

Laura's husband found her under the Marks's dining room table, kissing a dog on the lips.

"It's time to go," Edward said. She could smell his shoes—leather and old dirt. She imagined that if she were a dog, those smells would tell her every place he had been.

"This dog likes me," she informed him, and crawled out from under the table. She stood shakily, smoothing her green skirt.

He frowned at her, his eyes watering. He was allergic to dogs, and when he was around them too long his face puffed up like he'd been crying. "I can always tell when you've had too much wine, because you start stalking people's pets." He sounded more sad than disapproving.

It was true. After about four glasses of wine, Laura lost interest in human company and set about befriending the animal inhabitants. Once she had followed around a snarling white cat for nearly an hour, until the cat clawed her on the cheek (Laura was bent down, cooing at it) and drew so much blood that she had to ask her hostess for Band-Aids.

Edward led her by the elbow to the Marks's living room, where the remaining two guests (a couple of male professors, one of philosophy, one of French; Laura hadn't decided yet whether they were lovers, and if they were, whether or not anyone was supposed to know) were shrugging on their leather jackets. Emily and Benjamin Marks were smiling pleasantly, their eyes glazed. Laura imagined they would probably pass out while having sex.

"You know we're not supposed to *ask* certain questions," said Emily, a large-boned woman with shellacked white hair. "But it can't hurt to tell you things. Can it?" She giggled. She had the southern drawl Laura had been hearing all evening, but at least she could make out what Emily was saying. Earlier, a professor of theology had talked to her for nearly five minutes while she nodded and tried to follow what he was saying. It turned out that the only clear word, amidst the jangling drawl, was *Gawd*.

"What she's getting around to saying," said Benjamin, "is that we have a great school system and terrific churches. Unless you're Jewish." He held up a hand. "I'm not asking! I'm just informing you. We don't currently have a synagogue, but there is one just twenty miles down the road."

"Thank you," Edward said, and wiped at his eyes.

Laura pressed her lips together in what she hoped was a smile.

"Y'all have a good night now," Emily said, looking sweet and cross-eyed. "Are you gonna have time to go back to the motel before dinner?"

Edward looked at his watch. "Dr. Lewis is coming for us at seven," he said. "So yes."

Edward was interviewing for a job in the History Department. Today he'd taught a class on the Renaissance while Laura had driven the rental car through town, trying to imagine herself living here, in a Mississippi town she'd never heard of before. She drove through residential areas where purple flowers draped themselves over trees—wisteria, Benjamin Marks had told her this evening, it blooms every March—and sneezed until she had to roll up the windows. And wasn't the South supposed to be full of skinheads and debutantes? She'd seen one Confederate flag bumper sticker and resisted the impulse to give the driver the finger.

At home in New Hampshire, snow still covered their backyard and more was predicted for tomorrow. She loved snow, and she had said this to Emily Marks, who threw back her head and laughed. "It snowed here once, five years ago," Emily had told her. "Half an inch. And all the schools closed down!" When Emily had asked Laura what she did in New Hampshire (in a whisper, adding, "I'm not actually supposed to ask that"), Laura said she worked as a high school guidance counselor, leaving out the part about having just been fired.

Back at the Comfort Inn, Milo the cat was purring on Laura's suitcase, and the room smelled like piss.

"Fucking Milo," Laura cried, stomping toward him. He leapt into the closet and growled.

The only animal Laura did not like—hated, actually—was Milo, Edward's yellow cat. He had belonged to Edward's first wife, Glynnis. Glynnis took a teaching job in Japan and told Edward she was going to give Milo to the Humane Society. But Edward agreed to take him.

"He's just not used to motel rooms," Edward said, running water over some towels.

Usually, when they went away on trips, one of the high school students fed Milo, but those days were over.

Laura lay back on the bed, under a pastel watercolor of a magnolia tree. "We have great *schools* and *churches*," she said. "I don't think I want to go to dinner. I think I'm too tired to deal with any more prying answers to questions we don't want to ask."

Edward was dabbing at the floor with the towels. "I wish you'd go. Dr. Lewis is bringing his wife along. I think she's some kind of architect."

Laura closed her eyes. Why couldn't Edward have gotten an interview at Yale or Harvard or Boston College, or even someplace exotic, like Hawaii? She had encouraged him to apply everywhere, even places like North Dakota and Idaho. Even Mississippi. But this was the only interview he got. He didn't have many publications, which he blamed on the rigorous schedule of adjunct teaching, but Laura had seen his student evaluations: "Dr. Jenkins is probably a smart guy, but he's so boring I couldn't pay attention!" "Dr. Jenkins sucks." "Dr. Jenkins has NO redeeming qualities!!" One student had written only, "He is a nice dresser."

The truth about Edward was that he could be boring about the things he loved; unless, as Laura found out, the thing he loved was her. That was never boring. When he focused his attention on her, she didn't care what he said, or how he dressed.

"Just tell them I don't feel well," Laura said now. "Tell them I have to stay here and worship the devil."

Edward came over to her and pulled her shoes off. "I'll say you had a long day. Do you want me to bring you something from the restaurant?"

Bring me some other life, she thought, but she told him she'd just order pizza.

When he was gone, she threw Milo into the bathroom and shut the door, and then she tried to open the windows but they wouldn't budge. The room still stank.

Glynnis, Milo's previous owner, had been Laura's advisor at the University of New Hampshire. She had invited the students to her house at the end of the semester for a barbecue. That was where Laura had first seen Edward, standing at the grill in long blue shorts that made his legs look like white stalks of asparagus.

"That's my husband," Glynnis said. "He's studying for his PhD in history."

Laura's first thought was, How come someone as dweeby as him ended up with someone as cool as her? It didn't make sense.

That was also where she first met Milo, who spat at her.

Early the following fall, when Laura had started working at a high school in Dover, she ran into Edward in a Portsmouth coffee shop. He was sitting in a far corner, with papers spread around him, frowning and scribbling. When he saw her staring at him— she was staring both because he looked so frantic and because he seemed vaguely familiar—he lifted his hand and said, "Hey, Laura." And smiled at her.

"I don't want to interrupt you," she said, because she really didn't. She wanted to sit by herself and stare out the window at the rain and try to forget about the students who came to her office with their addictions and their eating disorders and their bruises. "It's not like I hate the job," she found herself saying, when he'd cleared a space for her, "but sometimes I just want to cry, you know? I didn't realize how fucked up some of these kids would be."

"But you're helping them," Edward said.

"I'm trying to help them, anyway." She stared at her cappuccino. "How's Glynnis?"

"She's fine. She left me." He said this calmly, stirring his coffee. "She got a job offer at the University of Tokyo and said that if I didn't want to go, that was fine with her." He shrugged. "I guess I didn't much want to go after that."

Laura felt the way she did earlier that day when a kid told her his father beat him. She felt small and powerless. Her mind could simply not fathom people who seemed so unreasonable, like the boy's father. Like Glynnis. To the kid in her office, she had said, "I think you should probably go to the nurse's office and get checked out." To Edward, she said, "I'm really sorry."

A year later they were married. That was four years and two pregnancies ago.

Now she flipped through the cable channels until she found an A&E special on serial killers. Milo was screaming in the bathroom; it sounded like he was throwing himself against the wall. His screams turned to low yowls.

"I know how you feel," she said. "But I still hate your guts."

She wanted to smoke, something she had stopped more than a year ago and then started again in the last few months. Along with drinking too much wine and making out with people's pets. "You need to take care of yourself," Edward warned her. "So we can try again."

Glynnis hadn't wanted children.

But things had turned out the way they were supposed to, hadn't they? Glynnis was supposed to pack up for Asia. Laura was supposed to marry Edward; they were supposed to make a family together.

Laura pulled a pack of cigarettes from her duffel bag—she had purchased them this afternoon, at a BP station, then made sure to hide them in her bag in case Edward went rooting through her purse again, busting her for smoking.

Outside, it had turned cool and the sky was the color of rotting grapes. The air smelled like exhaust and fast food. There was an Arby's across the parking lot, and a Movie Gallery, and Food Max. The road looked busy, but it still didn't lead anywhere. All the towns on the map had names that seemed like jokes: Hot Coffee. Gunville. Philadelphia. Houston. You had to drive three hours to get to Memphis, six hours to New Orleans. When the plane had circled low over the airport, Laura had looked out the window and thought: We're in the middle of fucking nowhere.

She sat down on the concrete steps and blew smoke into the air. If she was at dinner right now with Edward, she would be sitting there like a well-behaved wife, trying to make small talk with Mrs. Head of the Department, and she would be hating Edward. Right now she didn't hate him, not really, but she knew she could not, would not, live in this town.

A door opened a few rooms down and a girl slammed out of it, pulling on a denim jacket. She looked like she was about eighteen; her nose and eyebrow were pierced, and she wore a black tank top featuring Jesus in a Santa hat. She stared at Laura, narrowing her eyes, and stomped toward her so quickly that Laura thought she might step on her. But the girl stopped.

"Can I have one?" she said, pointing at the cigarette, and then plopped down next to Laura on the steps without waiting for an answer. "I'm going fucking insane in there. I had to get out."

Laura handed her a cigarette. She was hoping the girl would take it and leave, but she just sat there, gumming it, then asked, "Light?"

Laura handed her the lighter. The girl looked at her, waiting for some response.

Finally, Laura said, "Where are you going?"

The girl shrugged, squinting through the smoke. "I don't know. There's a bar up the street." She blew smoke at Laura. "You coming or what?"

The girl had a southern accent, but she didn't look like anybody Laura had seen around town, with her scowl and pierced eyebrow and her lank hair. She had the urge to say, "You ain't from these parts, are you?" but decided against it.

"Um," she said instead. "Okay. I'll drive."

The girl's name was Patty, and she was much older than she looked: twenty-six. She was interviewing at the university to be a post-doc in engineering.

"It's more like I'm interviewing *them*," she told Laura. They were sitting at the bar, with whiskey sours and hamburgers in front of them. The bar was attached to a bowling alley, which was attached to a strip mall. "I've got offers from all over, but my parents live here, and they said they'd babysit." Patty dug through her wallet to produce a picture of a red-haired toddler.

"Cute," said Laura, staring long at the picture. What would it be like to bring up a child in this nowhere town?

"Luckily she looks like me, and not like my ex-husband, David-the-Shit. You got kids?"

Laura examined her stirrer and was surprised to see that it had teeth marks on it. "Right now," she said, "I have a cat named Milo, which I hate. Edward refuses to put him in a kennel and our cat sitter was out of town. I was hoping he'd suffocate in the baggage compartment, but no such luck."

Patty was smiling at her, as if she'd just said something funny. "I bet you'd be good with kids," she said, and Laura was surprised to realize she seemed to be serious.

Laura was a good listener. That's what Edward told her, that's what the students who cried in her office told her. Sometimes kids who had cried in her office one semester came back a year later just to chat, to show off how well-adjusted they had become. She felt both pleased and worried about these students. "I'm glad you're doing so well!" she told them, but she was thinking: You're only seventeen, and your problems are still so small.

Kayla Lopez was a Hispanic girl who had transferred from a high school in Arizona. She had been sent to Laura's office for beating up a girl who had said, "Hey Lopez, where's your Chihuahua?" Kayla sat in the chair across from Laura with her fists clenched and her eyes narrowed.

According to her file, forwarded from her guidance counselor in Arizona, Kayla's father had left when she was four and she had a tendency toward pathological lying. *Needs to manage her anger*, said the file.

"I couldn't help it," Kayla said. "She was practically asking me to punch her. Don't you think?"

Laura waited for something wise to occur to her. Students often misinterpreted her silence as agreement, and this happened with Kayla now.

"You do think it! You just can't say it!"

"Hmm," said Laura, stalling. In her classes, Glynnis had put them into groups and had them videotape each other role-playing. Laura had always preferred to be the one making up problems for other people to solve.

"I hate my life," Kayla said. "You have no idea. I hate this shit hole of a town. I hate that my friends live in Arizona, and everyone here is a dumbass." She glared at Laura. "Including you. Sitting there like you know what you're doing."

If Glynnis were videotaping her now, Laura had no idea what she might say. But since she wasn't being videotaped, and since Kayla seemed on the verge of standing up and walking out—as if she were the one in charge—Laura decided to speak the truth.

"That girl," Laura told Kayla, "is an asshole to everybody. I'm supposed to tell you not to do it again—and you'd better not—but she had it coming."

Kayla relaxed a little. "So are you going to write me up or whatever?"

"You're already written up. You're already suspended for two days, and there's nothing I can do about that. I'm just here to talk to you about. . . ." She hesitated. Kayla was laughing.

"I know," said Kayla. "About my anger."

"Right," said Laura.

"I'll tell you what," Kayla said, leaning forward in her chair. "If anybody messes with me again, I'll—"

"Wait!" said Laura. "If you threaten anybody, I will have to report it. So watch what you say."

"Fine," said Kayla. "I get it."

"So maybe we'll be neighbors," Patty said. "We can hang out."

"Maybe," said Laura doubtfully.

Patty sucked her drink through her stirrer, then pointed it at Laura. "You should meet my ex-in-laws," she said. "Talk about crazy hicks. When David-the-Shit and I were in Italy for our honeymoon, he bought them an alabaster statuette of David. He wanted it because, you know, his name is also David. That's how conceited he was. Anyway, they magic-markered underwear on him!"

"No," said Laura.

"Swear to God," said Patty. "Oh, I could tell you stories about them. What're your in-laws like?"

"Dead," said Laura. "Everybody in both our families is pretty much dead."

"Lucky," said Patty.

The bar was filling up quickly, and the bartender—a goateed boy in a baseball cap—was ignoring them in favor of the tank-topped sorority types trying to squish their way in between Laura's and Patty's chairs.

"Ow," said Laura, when a girl beaned her with her elbow.

The girl tossed her hair and waved a twenty at the bartender.

"At least I won't have to worry about running into these bimbos," Patty said around the girl's chubby back. "You don't get many bimbos in engineering. Much to the dismay of the other engineers."

The girl gave them a nasty look and juggled her Jägermeisters out of the way.

"Where are you from?" Laura asked, but Patty was waving frantically at the bartender.

"Hey! Dude!" she screamed. The boy looked over. "Two more drinks!" She leaned back again. "What?" she said to Laura. "Oh, Heidelberg." She rolled her eyes. "A pit."

"But." Laura was confused. "When did you come to this country? I mean, that's amazing. Do you speak German?" She was imagining little Patty wandering through medieval streets.

Patty gave her a blank look, then burst out laughing. "Heidelberg, Mississippi," she said. "It's near Laurel."

Kayla was the kind of girl Laura would have been afraid of in high school, tough and smart and big. She wore oversized sweatshirts that said things like *#1 Goddess* and *Queen of the World*. Sometimes she wore them inside out.

Laura found herself looking forward to Kayla's appointments. "It's nice to finally get to talk to someone who actually has interesting problems," she told Edward. "I'm so sick of those skinny crying girls who think they're too fat, and the dumb-ass boys who won't lay off the pot long enough to lift a pencil."

Kayla didn't think she had any problems; she just came to Laura's office because her teachers kept sending her there. "You wrote your composition about a girl named Shayla who was molested by her uncle in Arizona," Laura said. "That's why your teacher was concerned."

Kayla rolled her eyes. "It's not a composition, it's a short story. It's fiction." She sounded like she was about thirty, talking to a three-year-old.

Laura frowned at her. "*Were* you molested by your uncle?"

Kayla just stared at her, smiling. "Isn't that in a file somewhere? If it's not, it must not have happened."

Laura paused. Kayla, she was realizing, was not a person who would fall for her wise silent routine. While other kids would burst into tears if Laura just smiled at them, Kayla stayed stony faced. Laura said, "I'm not going to make you talk about anything you don't want to talk about. What do you want to talk about?"

Kayla wanted to talk about Laura. "I'll bet you live alone with ten cats," she said. "I'll bet your mother comes over every week with casseroles 'cause you can't cook. And I bet you hate your job."

"Actually," said Laura, "my life is none of your business."

"My mother hates her job, too. She's a prostitute."

"Your mother is a dental assistant."

"She gives blow jobs to the dentist. When he says, 'suction,' she gets right down to it."

Laura had stopped taking notes after the first session. By the third week in October, she was having a hard time pretending to care about any of the other students, the ones with poor attendance and bruises. She found herself thinking, to her own horror, that they should just grow up.

"The thing I couldn't stand most about being pregnant," Patty was saying, "was not being able to drink beer. I could do without everything else. Didn't even crave a cigarette, not once. But sometimes I would just cry because I couldn't have a goddamn beer."

"You can have one beer," Laura told her. "Just not a lot of beer." But she hadn't drank anything at all. She hadn't taken aspirin, or eaten shellfish. She had not taken allergy medicine, even when her sinuses were killing her. She had left the feta cheese off her Greek salads. When she miscarried after two months, she blamed herself anyway. Edward had canceled his classes for a whole week and stayed home with her, stroking her hair while she cried. When she came back to work, she hated her students even more.

"Well, drink up," Laura told Patty. "If the bartender will come near us again."

When Laura was in college, she never went to bars. She never went anywhere. She stayed home and took care of her mother, who was dying of breast cancer, and she got straight A's, and she didn't date. Her mother—who had been proposed to three times by the time she was twenty—fretted that Laura would never get married, that she would be alone forever. "At least I had three good years with your father," she said. "And ten with the man before your father."

"I met my ex in a bar," Patty was saying. "In New Orleans. We were both there for spring break, and I flashed my boobs at him. I thought he was cute."

"My husband wants to divorce me because I drink too much," Laura said. This wasn't entirely the truth; she didn't think he wanted to divorce her. He just wanted her to be someone else. Someone who could cry at the right times and who didn't throw things when she got angry and who didn't leave parties to hunt down an animal to kiss.

"That's ridiculous," Patty said. "My ex could drink me under the table. That's where I flashed him, actually. Under a table."

Laura sighed. What had she been hoping? That Patty—wise, independent Patty—could actually tell her something she needed to know? She was just a person who didn't want to grow up. She was just one of those people who needed to make everything about herself.

"After I flashed him," Patty continued, "I puked on him. He cleaned me up and took me home and fucked me. It was romantic."

"I got fired because I hit a teenaged girl," said Laura, to see if she could get some reaction, but Patty was leaning away from her, pounding her empty glass on the bar.

Three years after her miscarriage, Laura got pregnant again. In her office one afternoon, she told Kayla that she would have to cancel their next appointment. "I have to go to the doctor," she said and felt herself blush. "I'm expecting." She was surprised to be telling Kayla this; the only other person who knew was Edward.

"Me, too!" Kayla cried. "I'm pregnant, too!"

Laura looked at her skeptically. "Are you sure? Who's the father?"

Kayla shrugged.

"Have you been to the doctor?"

"Sure," said Kayla.

Laura considered what to do. Of course Kayla was lying. Months went by and she didn't get any bigger. She talked about the baby, though, patting her flat stomach and saying things like, "She's going to grow up to be a porn star."

As they stood in the nursery, folding tiny T-shirts and socks into dresser drawers, Laura and Edward talked about William as if he were already a teenager causing trouble.

"What if he's gay?" Edward asked, looking down at her swollen belly.

"If he's gay, we'll be fine with it," said Laura.

"I just hope he doesn't start stealing cars."

"We'll give him a car as soon as he gets his license," said Laura. "And then he can be free to get a job at McDonald's."

"What if he wants to date someone outside of his religion?" Edward said.

"Thank God we don't *have* a religion!" Laura giggled. It was fun, making up their son.

He lived for three hours, fifty-six minutes, and twelve seconds.

When Laura returned to work two weeks later, Kayla sat across from her solemnly. Edward hadn't wanted her to back to work so soon, but Laura was sick of sitting around the house. They had given away the crib and the diapers, but the house still felt like it was waiting for something.

"I lost my baby," Kayla said.

Laura felt something inside her tearing or expanding, like the ghost of a contraction. She thought of the Winnie-the-Pooh mobile she had taken apart and put in the trash. "Kayla, you were never pregnant."

"I lost my baby!" Kayla said, and that was when Laura leaned over and slapped her across the face. Kayla stood up and walked out of the office. A few minutes later Mrs. Horowitz, the principal, barged into Laura's office, Kayla in tow.

"Did you hit this girl?"

Kayla was sobbing, she had bruises on her arms, a cut beneath her eye that was bleeding. She must have gone right into the bathroom and pinched herself, cut herself. "She threw a pen at me," Kayla said. "She grabbed me by my arms and shook me! Then she tried to scratch my eyes out."

"Yes," Laura said. "I did all those things. And I'd do it again."

Patty jumped off her bar stool and disappeared into the crowd, saying, "Fuck this waiting. I'll be back with more whiskey."

Laura's head was spinning. She thought of the rental car outside; three hours away were cities and lives she couldn't imagine. How many dark miles of highway could she put between herself and her own life? But even as she felt for her keys, she knew she would not try to find out. Edward would be back by now, would have found Milo in the bathroom, would have discovered her vanished, the rental car gone. He would be wondering if she had left him forever, and what he could have done to make her stay.

And when she got back to the motel, he would want to tell her how much he loved her, he would want to tell her about the head of the department and his architect wife, and about the life they could have here, and about trying again.

But for once, she wouldn't listen. "I can live here," Laura would tell him. "I can live anywhere. But I can not, I will not, try again."

Two days after she was fired, Laura had driven to Kayla's house. Her breasts had finally stopped leaking, but they were still tender. She wondered if they would ache forever.

Kayla's house was a beautiful three-story colonial, set back from the road behind oaks and ivy. Beside Laura on the front seat was a paper bag full of greeting cards she hadn't been able to bring herself to keep or to burn, cards that had been sitting in the bottom of her pajama drawer: *I am so sorry for your loss.* There was even one from Glynnis:

My thoughts and prayers are with you.

There wasn't much variety to sympathy cards.

Words can't say how sorry I am.

She had pushed the bag into the mailbox and then driven home shaking, the radio turned up full blast and pounding in her chest like another heart.

THE LAKE

Matthew's father calls to say, "I need my gun, the one in the basement behind the water heater."

"There's a gun in the basement?" Matthew asks. "*My* basement?"

"It's a Remington," his father says, as if there might be lots of guns behind the water heater. "I left it there when I moved out. I forgot about it till now."

"Is it loaded?"

"What use would it be if it wasn't?"

Matthew isn't sure what bothers him more—that his father had a loaded gun stashed in his house the whole time he'd been living there, or that he suddenly has a reason to need it.

"Is something the matter?" Matthew asks, not really wanting to know.

On the other end of the phone, 176 miles away, his father hesitates. "Bears," he says finally.

His father lives, for reasons Matthew can't comprehend, in a shack on the top of a mountain in western Maryland. He's taken partial retirement and with the money he claims to be saving on rent, he's bought himself a red Audi convertible for forty grand. Matthew knows, though his father has never come right out and said it, that the money is actually the last of what's left from selling the family house. His father had sold it ten years ago when Matthew's mother died; he'd then moved into a large, expensive apartment in Baltimore with a view of the Inner Harbor.

Matthew has long ago given up trying to understand his father.

"And listen," his father says. "I need you to bring the gun up here. I'm not going to be able to get out there, and I need it tomorrow."

Matthew lives in Fallston, a three-hour drive from his father's shack.

"Why? You're retired and it's Labor Day weekend. What do you have to do that's so important?"

"What do *you* have to do that's so important?" his father snaps.

Matthew's father thinks that since Matthew works at home writing grants, he has unlimited amounts of spare time. When he lived in Matthew's guest room, he was always making comments about how nice it must be to sit around all day.

"And another thing," his father continues. "You'd better bring your flashlight. I had the electricity turned off."

Matthew's wife, Saffron, thinks it's cute that his father lives in the woods. She's been asking Matthew for the past month when they're going to go visit. "It'll be like camping," she says. "We can do s'mores. I've always wanted to go camping and eat s'mores."

Saffron is a lawyer, an English girl Matthew met when they were both in law school at Johns Hopkins, before he flunked out. She grew up in a village where the milk was delivered in bottles and sheep wandered through the streets. She's enamored of all things American.

When Matthew tells her he's driving to see his father the next day, he doesn't tell her about the rifle. It was right behind the water heater like his father said it would be, but its appearance still shocked him for some reason—it wasn't hidden at all, just haphazardly stashed in such a way that if he or Saffron had turned on the overhead light they would have seen it. He'd picked it up, admiring the weight and heft of it, the cold smoothness. Then he'd aimed it at the clothesline, squinting, wondering what Saffron would do if she came down the stairs right then.

He tells Saffron his father has forgotten some shirts.

"But can't I come too?"

"It's not going to be a fun thing," he tells her. "No sing-alongs. No weenie roasts. I'm going to bring him his clothes and then turn around and come home."

"Well, bring him the mini fridge," says Saffron. "Make him use it."

"He doesn't have electricity," Matthew informs her. "He had it turned off."

"But if he has the fridge, maybe he'll *get* electricity."

Matthew sighs. "Sure," he says. "Maybe he will." He has no intention of trying to convince his father to get electricity. He's only agreed to go to his father's shack so he can take pictures of it and give them to his lawyer, as proof that his father is incompetent and should be put in a home. Not that he would tell Saffron this. Sometimes, Matthew thinks, people just don't know what's best for them.

The drive is surprisingly pleasant, the early September sun shining through the trees. It reminds Matthew of trips he and his sister took with their mother. Matthew's father had never shown an ounce of adventurousness. It was their mother who took Matthew and Nancy camping or fishing, or to the beach. Once, they had driven down to Virginia to hike the Appalachian Trail and camped for three nights.

Two months ago, Matthew called Nancy to inform her that their father had moved into a shack. Nancy said, "More power to him." Nancy lives in Chicago with her girlfriend, and she hasn't seen their father in ten years. The last time they were together as a family—at their mother's funeral—their father had made a deliberate point of ignoring Nancy's girlfriend.

"Don't you think it's weird that he's living like a fucking mountain man?" Matthew persisted. "Don't you think he's losing his mind?"

On the other end of the phone, he could hear Nancy exhale cigarette smoke. He pictured her in her high-rise, with its view of Lake Michigan. Not that she'd ever invited him to see it. "I don't care if he is or not," she said. "What does it matter, anyway? Aren't you just glad to have him out of your house?"

"Of course I am," Matthew said.

"So why not let him do his thing?"

Matthew couldn't come up with an answer.

Now, with the car windows rolled down, he wonders what will happen if he doesn't show up at his father's shack at all. In less than two hours—if he takes I-95 south instead of Route 70—he could be at his girlfriend, Alicia's, house in Georgetown. Sometimes he thinks of her as his girlfriend, even though they've never actually met. He imagines her opening the door and not recognizing him at first—they have, after all, only seen each other on their computer screens—and then she would bring him inside and tell him to stay as long as he likes.

It's even worse than he'd imagined. Twice he was convinced he was lost—his car maneuvered deep ruts and weeds rose up on all sides. How could this dirt road possibly lead anywhere? Human habitation seemed impossible. The sun bore down, and Matthew turned on the air conditioner. He had counted on the drive taking three hours, but he hadn't figured in the Labor Day traffic, and by the time he finds himself parked in front of his father's shack, it's nearly sundown.

He sits in his car for a moment, wondering if he should take a picture or wait. The house looks like something out of a bad movie, the kind of place where teenagers get hacked to death. The front porch sags; one of the front windows is covered in masking tape. His father's convertible is tarped and birds have pooped all over the black plastic. The air is turning nippy. Matthew had forgotten how fast the weather changes when you're in the mountains, how the sun can fall below the trees and the air turn cold in moments.

On one overnight camping trip with his sister and mother, Matthew had wandered out of the tent, thinking he heard someone calling his name. He realized it was a bird, an owl perhaps—but still, the forest seemed to draw him toward it, farther and farther, until he was lost and shivering, feeling foolish. He'd waited, wondering if his mother would come looking for him, then commenced calling for help: a high-pitched sound that embarrassed him. He was twelve. His mother found him what seemed like hours later but must have only been minutes, her flashlight hunting through the trees. When she grabbed him into her arms, he understood that she was the bravest person he would ever know.

There was never a question of his father going along. His father needed television and microwaved dinners and an adjustable chair. And now here he is, living the life Matthew's mother would have loved. But she would have insisted on electricity. She would have warm beds and a fire roaring and rugs on the floor.

"Bring your sleeping bag," his father had snapped on the phone. "And get here before dark."

"I'm not staying overnight with you," Matthew protested. "I'll get a motel room."

"No, you won't," said his father. "There's no motels around for miles."

Which Matthew had thought was a lie, but now he realizes it's true.

Matthew's father slams out the front door and stands on the porch with his hands on his hips, looking to Matthew like the villain in a bad movie: the one responsible for hacking those teenagers to death. In the two months since he's seen him, his father has grown a beard and an old-west handlebar mustache.

Matthew reluctantly gets out of his car and walks around to the back, where the gun is lying next to the mini fridge.

"I brought you a mini fridge," he says. "All you need now is electricity."

"Did you see the lake?" his father shouts, stalking over to Matthew. "It's a beautiful lake."

"I didn't see any lake."

His father grabs the gun and smiles at it like it's a long-lost friend.

"Be careful with that thing," Matthew tells him. "Do you even know how to use one of those?"

"Of course I do." His father sounds affronted. "My father used to take me hunting when I was a boy. Taught me how to shoot one of these babies."

"Is that the same gun?"

"No." His father glares, as if Matthew has just insulted him again. "You know, I would have taken *you* hunting, but your mother wouldn't let me." Then his eyes seem to cloud over, and he gazes mournfully into the distance. "The lake is on the other side of the ridge. We'll go tomorrow. Beautiful, that lake."

"Great," says Matthew. "So I should leave the mini fridge in the car?"

"I don't care what you do with it. Did you eat dinner?"

"I stopped in Cumberland and got something."

"Good." His father just stares at him, as if waiting for him to issue a challenge. "Come inside then. Don't just stand there like an idiot."

Matthew's father had lived with him and Saffron for four months, after he lost his job and couldn't pay rent on his expensive Inner Harbor apartment. He'd lost his job as customer relations manager at a phone company when he told a customer to go fuck himself. "People," he said to Matthew, "are too goddamn sensitive."

It was Saffron's idea that Matthew's father move in with them.

"But we don't even like each other," Matthew reminded her.

"He's not a bad guy," Saffron said.

"No," said Matthew. "He wouldn't visit my mother in the hospital when she was dying, but heck, that doesn't make him a bad *guy*."

Saffron rolled her eyes. "It makes him a jerk, so what? It makes him human."

No, thought Matthew. *That's not what makes people human.* But he let his father move in with them anyway.

"I'll stay out of your hair," his father had said. And then he proceeded to make his presence known in every annoying way: leaving the kitchen cabinets wide open, forgetting to flush the toilet, even—once—leaving the phone off the hook. Sometimes Matthew heard him wandering around in the middle of the night, creaking up and down the basement steps. And there was one time just before dawn when Matthew was almost certain he heard his father crying. After that, he wore earplugs to bed.

Even when the house was silent, his father might just as well have been screaming and slamming his fists against the wall. He might have been banging on their bedroom door like a poltergeist, demanding to be heard.

Matthew wakes up with a backache, needing coffee.

"I don't have any coffee," his father says. "I have tea." He's sitting in front of the fireplace, which looks like it hasn't been cleaned in twenty years. The house is one large room, with a cot in one corner, a blue card table, a throw rug that Matthew recognizes from the basement in the house where he grew up. There's a kerosene lamp by the door and a case of Diet Dr. Pibb on the floor next to a hot plate. A large mosquito hovers next to the window, trying desperately to escape. The place smells inexplicably like french fries, and then Matthew sees the McDonald's wrappers spilling out of a Hefty bag.

Matthew struggles up from the hard floor, bunching his sleeping bag and rubbing his neck. "But you always drink coffee! You can't *function* without coffee!"

It's the one thing they have in common.

His father is shaking his head. "Not anymore. I'm a tea man."

"Jesus." Matthew kicks at his sleeping bag. "I can't fucking believe this. If you'd told me that, I'd've brought my own."

His father shrugs, smiling the same shit-eating grin that Matthew has hated his whole life.

"All right," Matthew says. "You've got your gun. I'm heading home."

"I need to show you the lake." His father turns from the fireplace, and Matthew thinks he sees something like fear in his eyes. "It's a beautiful lake."

Matthew rubs his forehead. "I need to pee," he says.

His father points to the back of the cabin. "You gotta go around and up a little hill. There's an outhouse. You can't miss it. It's blue."

"Where on earth did you get an outhouse?"

"It was already here, what do you think?" says his father. "When you get back, we'll go to the lake. And then you can leave. Okay?"

Matthew feels like a hostage. He considers, as he treks up the hill to the outhouse, just making a run for it. But his keys are still in the cabin. And his camera. He needs to take pictures of the outhouse—cleaner than he'd expected, but still—and of the rotted planks in the porch. Matthew will feel much better knowing his father is someplace where people—people other than himself and Saffron—can keep an eye on him, keep him away from loaded guns and make him use an indoor toilet. He's a danger to himself, Matthew thinks. How could anyone argue with that?

His father's right about one thing: it *is* a beautiful lake. The midmorning sun shines on its flat surface, making Matthew think of those old Nestea plunge commercials. It would be a good place to swim in the summer. A good place to bring children. Above them, squirrels leap between trees, shaking the gold-edged leaves and floating some to the ground. A dragonfly hovers nearby, like a miniature helicopter.

"What'd I tell you?" says his father, taking a deep breath. "God's country." For some reason, he'd insisted on bringing his gun, which he's holding now.

"You don't believe in God," Matthew points out. "But yes. It's nice." He swats at a yellow jacket.

"Nice!" His father snorts. "It's better than nice."

Then they just stand there, staring toward the distant shore, until Matthew says, "Well, I'd better head back."

"I need to tell you something." His father is still looking into the distance. "I haven't seen any bears."

"Okay," says Matthew.

"I've seen something . . . out there." His father still isn't looking at him. "Some sort of . . . lake creature." Then he turns to Matthew, and Matthew sees that glimmer of fear again. "I almost said monster," he hurries on, "but I can't assume it means any harm. Maybe it's just some prehistoric creature that's trying to survive. But whatever it is, it's nothing I want crawling ashore." He shudders. "It was horrible. Long neck. Big eyes."

Matthew stares at his father. "You're kidding me."

"The first time I saw it was two weeks ago. I like to come out here on Saturday afternoons and fish—"

"You fish?" Matthew interrupts. "Since when do you fish?"

"Since I moved out here!" His father laughs. In the spackled sunlight, Matthew has a flash of what his father must have looked like as a little boy. "I was just standing here, fishing and thinking—"

"Thinking about what?" Matthew can't stop himself. He actually wants to know.

"Hell, I don't know. That's not the point! The point is that I saw something. It was in the middle of the lake." His father squints, pointing. "And it hardly made a ripple."

"Like the Loch Ness Monster?"

"Fuck the Loch Ness Monster! That was some guy with a hose. This was real."

"And you're afraid it's going to come onshore and do what?

"I don't know! How am I supposed to know that?" His father is angry, nearly stomping his foot. "How the hell do I know what it can do? It's not supposed to even exist!"

"But if it does come on land, you're going to shoot it."

"Or shoot at it. I don't have to kill it."

"Why?"

"It's probably as scared as we are."

Matthew looks into his father's wide brown eyes, searching for signs that he's joking. Once, when he was a child, his father had hidden under his bed until Matthew fell asleep, then started pushing at the bedsprings. Matthew had flown down the hall screaming. His father came out of his bedroom doubled over with laughter. Matthew's mother had marched out of the master bedroom, dragging the blankets behind her, and stayed with Matthew in his room until he fell back asleep.

His father isn't smiling now. He looks genuinely worried. "Anyways," he says, and clears his throat. "I was hoping you might see it too. It would make me feel better, knowing somebody else saw it."

Leaves rustle with another squirrel chase. Matthew has no idea what to say to his father.

This is what he's been looking for, proof that his father is losing his mind.

Finally, Matthew turns back toward the direction of the cabin and announces, "I'm driving into town for coffee."

He calls Saffron on his cell phone from the Safeway parking lot.

"He's lost it. He's seeing the Loch Ness Monster."

"How'd he like the fridge?"

"Did you hear me? He's seeing things."

"Oh, he's just teasing you."

Matthew pretends to consider this, but he is actually thinking that Saffron doesn't understand how the world works; she can spend her whole life ignoring what she doesn't want to think about. She can keep on believing that they're going to have a baby in a year, when they haven't had sex in six months.

"Well, I'm going to stay here another night, just in case."

He waits for her to say, "Just in case there *is* a monster? Are you crazy?" But all she does is sigh and say, "Please make him take the fridge. I don't want it anymore."

When Matthew's father first moved in with them, Saffron was the one who stopped wanting to have sex. "It's too strange," she whispered in bed the first night. "I'm afraid he might hear us."

"He's all the way down the hall," Matthew said. Then louder, "Dad? Can you hear me? Hey, Dad!"

"Shut up!" cried Saffron. They waited for a moment in silence; she had her head halfway under the covers, like a child.

"See?" Matthew said, after a moment. "We're good."

"No, I just can't." There were times when her accent charmed him and others when it annoyed him; this was one of the latter. She sounded absolutely prudish, like some Victorian woman afraid of piano legs: "I *cahn't*, I simply *cahn't*."

"Fine," Matthew muttered, and curled up with his back to her.

He doesn't think it's the lack of sex that drove him online to Alicia; it was feeling like a stranger in his own house. He was used to being alone all day—turning up the radio too loud, fixing grilled cheese sandwiches, and taking a lunch break to watch the news. With his father there, he felt caged and constantly annoyed.

Saffron was under the impression that Matthew and his father would spend much of the day in each other's company, talking and laughing and reminiscing about old times. She'd come home every evening with a look of childish anticipation on her face. While they were in the kitchen she'd whisper to Matthew, "*Well?*"

"Well, what? I worked and he stayed in his room, except to come out and watch some stupid game show."

Saffron frowned and shook her head, disapproving. "I just think you two should make the most of this opportunity," she said.

Matthew takes his father out to an early dinner at Red Lobster in the nearest town, ten miles away. They take Matthew's car, because his father is worried about somebody stealing the Audi.

"What's the point of having a forty-thousand-dollar car you won't drive?"

"Oh, I drive it. I just don't like to take chances."

They haven't spoken about the lake monster since that morning, but now Matthew looks at the menu and says, "Hmm, the monster looks good."

His father says nothing.

"I mean *lobster*."

"I know what I saw," his father says. He goes tight lipped and frowns over the menu as if it's full of secret codes.

Matthew sighs and shakes his head, an elaborate gesture that his father doesn't catch. But the cute waitress does, and she raises her eyes at him and smiles. What to make of that smile? Matthew smiles back at her, as if to say: *Fathers! What are you gonna do?*

She's coming toward them now, pen poised above a pad of paper, and Matthew takes this opportunity to say to his father, loudly, "Remind me to stay at a hotel next time!" He turns to the waitress. "My father lives in a shack out in the woods. No electricity. Can you believe it?"

He does not know what he's doing, nor can he stop.

"That sounds real nice," the waitress says. "Can I start you off with some iced tea or a margarita?"

"You from around here?" Matthew asks, still smiling, still aware of his father glowering behind the menu.

"Sort of," says the waitress, now slightly on her guard.

"Anybody ever see monsters in the lake? That you know of?"

She seems to consider this. "I heard about some UFOs a few years ago. But I think it turned out to be army planes."

Matthew's father clears his throat. "I want the iced tea and the shrimp combo," he says, and then gets up and heads toward the restroom. Matthew notices, for the first time, that his father moves stiffly, nearly limping.

"And you?" the waitress says. She's probably about eighteen, might have big dreams of going to the community college and getting a managerial job at Wal-Mart. If Matthew lived here, in this nowhere town, he'd probably keep coming back here and making an ass of himself.

Because of course, if he did live in this nowhere town, it would be because he and Saffron had separated. He can't imagine them divorced, but separated seems more and more likely.

When his father returns to the table, Matthew says, "Do you think Mom would believe you?"

"Your mother didn't need explanations. She was a trusting woman." He stares at the table. "I squandered my time with her," he says quietly.

"So now you're squandering her money? Buying a car you can't even drive? You could have given that money to me, you know."

And for an instant, Matthew thinks he understands his father, just a little—the old man is deliberately ruining his life. Out of some sense of guilt, perhaps? Matthew doesn't know, and he decides not to ask.

One warm April day when Matthew was fourteen, he decided to skip school and go fishing. It was the first time he'd lied to his parents, the first time he'd allowed himself entry into a world of unknown dangers. Not just the danger of being caught and punished, but of revealing who he really was: a boy who lied and loved it.

He took his paper bag of peanut butter sandwiches and carrot sticks, waved good-bye to his mother standing by the kitchen window, and then biked off toward school. His mother must have been forty then, and she looked like a teenager. Her hair was carrot-red, and her face was round and freckled. His father had left for work an hour earlier, and Nancy was off at college, a world Matthew had no interest in imagining.

He took a shortcut, on a dirt road that went past the cornfield, and he came across two bicyclers taking up the road—a man and a woman, steering like they were drunk, weaving all over the place and laughing like lunatics. The woman had long blonde braids and Matthew only recognized the man as his father—he was wearing a red baseball cap Matthew had never seen before—from his voice booming out, "Wait, honey! Slow down!"

Did his father see him? Or did Matthew fly by so quickly as to be nearly invisible?

His father came home that night as usual from the advertising job he'd had for eighteen years. He was wearing his gray business suit and carrying his briefcase, frowning and grumbling and asking for a beer, and when Matthew's mother said, "How was work?" his father muttered fine, and Matthew could not for the life of him tell if anything was different.

But then, his father might be wondering the same thing about him, mightn't he? Did he know that Matthew had seen them? All through dinner, Matthew could not stop thinking about the woman with the blonde braids: Who was she? It would have made more sense if he'd seen them kissing—but riding bicycles? His father didn't even own a bicycle.

He started to doubt his own memory, until about five years later—he was home from college for Christmas—his parents had a party and the woman was there. Her hair was short now and she was with her husband, a man his father introduced as his boss.

Matthew got drunk that night. He can't be sure exactly what he said, because he never asked, but he is certain it was something terrible. He remembers his mother's face going slack and the blonde woman starting to cry, and his father slamming out of the house. He remembers, the next morning, throwing up in the trash can while his mother packed her things—slowly, meticulously, one suitcase after another. Where did she get so many suitcases? He remembers her getting in her car, and kissing him good-bye, and telling him to call her at her sister's house in Richmond. His own sister had begun slipping away from the family by then, spending the holidays at some friend's house.

Later, his father would either quit his job or be fired—Matthew never asked—and go on unemployment for a few months before beginning the first of many low-paying, dead-end jobs.

Matthew remembers his father staring at him from the living room sofa the day after the party, sitting there with one leg thrown over the other, the television blasting some damned parade—just staring until Matthew got in his own car and drove away.

"When did you buy the gun?" They're back in Matthew's car, headed toward the cabin. It's early evening, the sun glaring through the trees.

"You and Nancy and your mother were camping one weekend . . . I think it was the time you hiked the Appalachian Trail." His father is staring straight ahead, as if making sure Matthew knows where he's going. "Remember that?"

Matthew remembers.

"And I woke up in the middle of the night, and someone was trying to break into the house."

"Are you sure?"

"Sure I'm sure! I *saw* the guy, outside the dining room window! I called the police, but by the time they got there, the guy was gone."

"But . . . you never said anything."

"Didn't want to scare you. But the next day I bought the rifle, kept it hidden under the bed."

"So you bought a *Remington*? Why not a handgun?"

"I *like* Remingtons!" his father booms. He looks like he wants to jump right out of the car. "I told you that."

"And Mom never found it."

"Nope."

But she would have found it, Matthew knows. When she was packing her things and moving out, she would have found it, and there would have been another fight. Matthew is suddenly certain that his father is lying about the gun, that he bought it after his mother was gone. That he didn't mean to use it on any burglars.

A danger to himself, Matthew thinks, and remembers all the nights when his father had creaked up and down the basement steps. "What's he doing?" Saffron had whispered, but Matthew had pretended to be asleep. He never asked her if she thought she heard his father sobbing, and she never mentioned it.

When they get back to his father's house, the sun is nearly down and Matthew is exhausted. He hates the idea of the three-hour-drive home, but mostly he hates the thought of what will happen when he gets there. He imagines Saffron's face eager and expectant: *What happened? Was it fun?*

His father lights the kerosene lantern and the house fills with shadows. Then he settles down on the floor and spreads out the McDonald's he'd insisted they pick up at a drive-thru on the way home. He'd barely touched his Red Lobster food.

"You should get chairs," Matthew tells him.

"Don't need them," says his father, biting into a Big Mac.

"Well, do you have any booze?" Matthew asks, and is surprised when his father pulls a nearly full bottle of Maker's Mark from under the cot. *Since when do you drink alone?* Matthew wants to say, but he doesn't.

Now is the moment, in Saffron's scenario, when they would get drunk and cry and hug, but they don't. They eat their french fries and drink from chipped tea cups and finally his father says, "I'm hitting the sack." He steps outside to brush his teeth in the hose water that—Matthew was mortified to learn—also serves as his shower. How long can a person live this way? What will happen when winter comes?

His father stomps back inside, kicks off his shoes, and curls up on the cot. "Turn off the kerosene before you go to sleep," he says, and hunches toward the wall.

On the day Matthew's mother went to the hospital with stomach pains—barely a year after she had moved out—Matthew's father called him at college. "I think your mom's pretty sick," he said.

She had moved back to Maryland, but into her own apartment. She had filed for divorce by then, but his father was refusing to sign the papers.

"Yeah? Like, appendicitis or something?"

"Like, the doctor thinks she has cancer. Or something."

It was a Friday night, nine o'clock. Matthew had five shots of Cuervo in him and a date with a girl in his French class. They were going to go clubbing in Baltimore. The girl had short brown hair and a mouth like Julia Roberts's. The University of Maryland was forty miles away from where his mother lay in the hospital, less than an hour on I-95. "I'll be there tomorrow," Matthew said. "My car's broke down, but I'll get it fixed tomorrow . . . or I'll borrow somebody's car. I'll get there somehow." He wondered if his father knew he was lying, if he knew somehow that Matthew was too drunk and too scared to get in the car.

"Your sister's flying in tomorrow," his father said, and that was when Matthew really felt afraid, through the haze of tequila and the buzzing of lust for the girl he was going to meet that night. His sister didn't come home for anything.

Later, he would tell Saffron, on their second date: "My father never even visited my mother in the hospital. She went in on a

Friday night and I got there on Saturday, and my dad was sitting outside in the lobby afraid to go in. She died a week later on the operating table."

"He was just afraid," she said. "He couldn't bear to see the woman he loved die."

"No," said Matthew, thinking of the hospital lobby with its cold blue walls and its televisions playing laugh tracks. "He was a coward. We never talk about it."

While his father sleeps, Matthew pours himself more Maker's Mark and allows himself to consider the scenario that, while he's been gone, Saffron has been snooping through his computer, discovering that he's been chatting online with a girl named Alicia who sends him pictures of herself naked. He allows himself to consider this only because he doesn't consider it an actual possibility. For one thing, Saffron isn't exactly computer savvy. For another, she has no reason to suspect such a thing. Yes, Matthew spends long hours in the middle of the night sitting at his desk in the study (or, when his father was there, the living room), but most of that is legitimate work. He finds it easier to work in the middle of the night, when the house is so still he can hear the buzz of every appliance, the tick of every clock.

Lately he's been taking chances, leaving the screen up when he leaves his desk. Just last week he'd stood paralyzed by the refrigerator as, at 2:30 in the morning, he heard Saffron tiptoe down the hall. All she had to do was look in the study—but she went straight to the kitchen and put her arms around him, nudged her soft head under his chin, held him for a full minute, and walked back down the hall to their bedroom.

One night several months ago, he'd been sitting in the living room, talking quietly to Alicia through the webcam. She was naked and smiling, rubbing her breasts, and he was holding his penis in his hand, and it took him a moment to understand what she was saying: "Do you think he likes this, too?" He turned around and his father was standing there in the doorway, looking as if he'd been slapped. He turned and went back down the hall to his room, and three days later he said he was moving out.

When Matthew hears his father's breathing grow slow and steady, punctuated by brief snorts, he rises and puts on his jacket and takes the flashlight from the table next to the door. Outside, the wind is stirring and an owl—Matthew thinks it's an owl—flashes through the trees. The darkness is so thick he can feel it on his face; he almost doesn't want to turn on the flashlight, but he does so he can make his way through the brambles, toward the lake. How far can he walk without knowing where he's going?

When he sees the lake, he feels his heart catch—the moon is gliding on the water, melting across it. For reasons he can't begin to understand, Matthew suddenly wants to weep. He stares hard, willing himself to see something. And for a moment, he *does* see it, glistening as it rises out of the dark water. A long neck, like a magnificent horse. Fear gallops through him; he feels blessed, then cursed, and just as he's wondering if there are other lies he can make true, a gunshot reverberates through the trees behind him.

Matthew's mother spent what would be the last year of her life moving out of the house, hiring a lawyer, finding an apartment. Sometimes she would call him in the middle of the night, sobbing. "What did I do wrong, Matty? Do you know what I did wrong?"

"Nothing," he told her. "Nothing."

"I was a fool," she said. "I'm too old for this."

"It was one summer," Matthew's father told him. "One summer, a long time ago. Your mother and I still loved each other!" *Until you ruined it.* He didn't say this, but there it was.

Later, Matthew wanted to ask his father: Did she forgive you? Does she forgive me? But of course, he never did.

He wanted to ask her himself, but he never could. He never stepped foot in her hospital room, while his father and sister sat by his mother's bed.

He hates the lie he told Saffron, hates that he'd claimed it was his father who had been the coward. And he hates that there is so much to be sorry for that he couldn't say he was sorry at all.

His father says, "I scared it pretty bad." He's walking slowly from the trees, his face pale in the moonlight. "May have even nipped it a little." His hands are shaking so badly he can hardly hold the gun. Matthew takes it from him. The smell of gunpowder still hangs in the trees, and Matthew has the strange feeling that his heart has broken apart and is floating through the air, trying to find its way back to him.

His father's eyes are wide and moist. "I thought it was going to take you."

As they walk back to the cabin in silence, Matthew realizes he's trembling. In the few seconds between the gunshot and his father appearing from behind the trees, Matthew had been certain that his father had brought him here to witness the end of a ruined life. And he, Matthew, had come here as a willing accomplice, driving nearly two hundred miles with a loaded gun in his car, for his father.

Back inside, with the kerosene lamp burning, Matthew helps his father start a fire in the fireplace. They work silently, crumbling newspaper, arranging logs.

"I was thinking I nearly saw something out there," Matthew says.

"It's gone for now."

"Okay," says Matthew. The next day, he knows, he will drive home, and he will tell himself he didn't see anything, and by the time he gets home it will seem like a dream. He won't tell Saffron what he saw. "I'm pretty sure I did," he says after a long silence. "See something, I mean. I don't know what it was, but I saw it. I really did." The more he says it out loud, the more he knows it to be true.

His father doesn't answer. They settle down cross-legged to stare at the fire and wait for morning.

SECRETS OF OLD-TIME SCIENCE EXPERIMENTS

Aunt Julep returned after two years, slapping up our dusty driveway in the same pink slippers she'd run away in. She hauled a battered yellow suitcase by its rainbow strap with one hand; with the other she dragged a brown-and-white beagle on a snarled old rope. Her hair, which I remembered as coarse and white and always clamped tightly to her head, was flying in her face like a swarm of dragonflies.

My sister, Nellie, and I were squatted on our front walk, maneuvering Barbie up the drainpipe. "A puppy!" screamed Nellie, who was too young to remember Aunt Julep. Barbie clattered to the sidewalk with her tutu bunched up around her waist.

The dog yelped and Aunt Julep let the rope fly out of her hands and set the suitcase down with a loud "humph" sound.

"Hello, Louise. Hello, Nellie." She sat down on the suitcase with some difficulty, and when she dragged off her camel-colored jacket I could see why: Aunt Julep was wrapped up tightly in a red kimono. It was knotted precisely at her middle, like a poppy blooming from her belly button.

"We're exploring caves," I said, groping around for Barbie, trying not to stare.

"I can see that," said Aunt Julep. She spit a piece of hair from her mouth. "Nellie, honey, don't sit on Puppy, he's not a horse." Then, tilting her round chin to the sky, she held out both red arms in front of her, like a zombie or a sleepwalker. I thought she'd gone into one of her trances and was making for the front door when she crooked a finger at me. "Louise, be a sweetheart and haul an old lady to her feet."

Aunt Julep wasn't our real aunt. I was only nine the last time I saw her, but I remembered that much. She'd rented our upstairs apartment, which was directly over my room. At night, I could hear music and the shuffling of feet and Aunt Julep's laughter rolling from wall to wall. I had once snuck upstairs when she was out shopping, but all I could see through the keyhole was a purple sweater drying on the radiator. When I told my mother about the dancing and the music, she said that Aunt Julep was a lonely old woman who liked to think about the past, and who could blame her, with a past like hers?

Aunt Julep was the daughter of a magician, the great Dr. Fenworth, renowned mesmerist and levitationist and table rapper. She had traveled around with him as his assistant, going into trances and speaking in tongues. She could float across the room, flat as a board, her eyes rolled back to show the whites. She'd once shown me a picture of herself as a child. She was wearing something called a sari, reclining on her side in midair while Dr.

Fenworth waved a black wand at her. Once, she was proud to tell us, she had made ectoplasm come right out of her ear. It had looked like Susan B. Anthony. ("Not a lot of people recognized her. But the ones who did were mightily impressed.") When she was older, young men tried to woo secrets from her. Instead, she read their palms and predicted death by drowning for each and every one. She had once promised to read my fortune but had somehow never gotten around to it.

One morning at breakfast she ran away, throwing the rent check at my mother and dragging her suitcase clompedy-clomp down the porch steps, shouting that she'd had a vision: Her dear pappy needed her. She scrambled into her orange Bronco and bounced off down our driveway, leaving a trail of whirling dust.

"You lucked out, Julep," said my mother, leading the way up the narrow stairwell to the attic. I followed Julep's red satin behind, which smelled faintly of cinnamon, faintly of damp dog. "The boy who was renting from us went off to grad school in Boise, and we haven't had time to find someone else. So it looks like you've got your old place back." My mother had been rooting around in some top cabinets when we came inside, and she nearly toppled off the step ladder when she saw Julep standing in the kitchen. "I'm trying to find the thyme," she had said, as if she were the one who had some explaining to do.

"Time for what?" Julep said. Inside, standing on linoleum among the mundanities of appliances, she had looked even stranger than she had out in the driveway.

"As you can see," said my mother now, jiggling the key in the lock and swinging the door open, "we've done some painting, and we've put in a microwave. And Bill left his lamp, so you can have that, too."

"Marvelous," Julep cried, clapping her hands.

"You didn't used to have a dog," said my mother tactfully.

Julep wandered over to the window and heaved it open. Nellie and Puppy were howling on the grass below, and Julep leaned so far over the ledge that my mother stepped forward in alarm. "Puppy loves children," Julep said, ducking back inside. "He's actually a direct descendant of Mini, who was part of my father's act back in the 1920s. After the accident—" she brought a plump hand to her throat—"I kept Puppy, and he's really helped me get through it all." She bowed her head.

My mother came over and put her arm around Julep's shoulder. Julep snuffled and I looked away, embarrassed. "We read about your father in the newspaper," said my mother gently, guiding Julep over to the tiny kitchen table and easing her carefully into a chair. "What happened?"

"It was a terrible thing," said Julep, recovering. She wiped a red satin arm across her upper lip. "He was nearly ninety, you know, and still doing those escapes from trunks and tanks of water, although they took him longer and longer and he nearly drowned more than once. His grand finales had gone steadily downhill. I remember when he used to be locked in a sarcophagus, set afire, and suspended in midair! And he'd come bounding out from the wings just when you were sure he'd finally had it this time. But in his last days, all he could manage to escape from were ordinary storage trunks—not that there's anything to be ashamed of there, considering he was nearly ninety."

"Of course," said my mother.

"He had this trick where he would climb into a trunk and then crawl through a secret door to reappear on the other side of the stage. Then when his assistant opens up the trunk—ta-da! It's empty. Then he would come leaping out of the wings and the crowd would go wild—partly, I think, because they had never seen a man so old *leaping* before. And then"—she took a breath—"he got in there and finally forgot how to get out. So Teresa—his assistant—opens up the trunk and ta-da! There he is, huddled up in a little ball, scared as a baby. I think it was the humiliation that killed him more than anything else. And I, as you can imagine, was positively devastated. I just set off traveling, first to the Orient, then Egypt, then to India—did a bit of snake charming there, fascinating place."

My mother cast a nervous glance toward Julep's yellow suitcase.

"How come you weren't your father's assistant anymore, Aunt Julep?" I asked, flopping out on the sofa bed.

Julep's gray eyes flickered like crystal balls. "People want to see an old man escape from a trunk, because they think it's heroic," she said evenly, baring her small white teeth in what could have been a smile. "But no one wants to see a fat old woman hovering in midair, chanting in Mandarin Chinese. It's not magic anymore; it's a freak show."

I didn't hear any music coming from Julep's apartment this time, or any dancing feet. Just the flat-footed shuffle of Julep in her pink slippers. She put away her kimono and dressed in muted pastel pantsuits—pink, mostly, but sometimes baby blue. She secured her wild white hair in a sensible knot at the back of her neck.

Instead of telling us stories about her adventures as a magician's daughter, she started doing grandmotherly things that she hadn't done before— baking cookies with me, helping my mother in the garden, reading Dr. Seuss to Nellie. She even went so far as to darn my father's socks.

"You *darned* my socks? I don't even know what darning is, but my socks are good as new. Thank you, Julep." He was blushing. My father didn't like people to do things for him; he said it made him feel in their debt. But I also know that his mother had died when he was a teenager, and Julep brought out a boyishness I'd never seen in him before. He showed her the fancy tricks he could do on his computer, and Julep said that what her father did was nothing compared to magic like this. And everyone agreed that Puppy was well behaved and intelligent, just the kind of dog anyone would be glad to have. Nellie had taught him to shake hands.

My parents called Julep a godsend and didn't charge her rent after the first month. They said that time and travel can certainly change a person, and that her father's death—while tragic—had alerted her to the Things That Are Really Important. Things like family—which, lucky us, we had become.

She ate meals with us and went to church with us, and on Christmas she gave us all sweaters she'd made herself. Then she surprised my parents with guitars. "I know how important your music used to be to you," she told them, pooh-poohing their cries of protest. "I used to listen to your records over and over And I think it's a shame that you don't play any more; you really should."

Before they were my parents, Ellen and Marvin Linder were a singing sensation known as the Marv-Els. They'd traveled around the country, playing in coffee houses and opening for larger acts, and had released two albums, which were stashed in the credenza in the dining room. After Julep gave them the guitars, they brought out the records and began playing their old songs and writing new ones. They played at the community college and at weddings, and in April, my father made an important announcement at dinner. He was holding a big white envelope.

"You're not going to believe this, but we're being offered an incredible amount of money to go on a reunion tour."

"How much?" asked my mother. My father told her, and her fork clattered to the floor.

"Well, you must go, that's all there is to it," said Julep, dabbing the side of her mouth with her napkin, "and I'll take care of the children. No, no—" She held up her hand. "I insist."

"We'll pay you, of course," said my father, relenting.

"Not at all," said Julep. "You two just go and have a wonderful time, and don't worry about a thing. Louise and I can hold down the fort, can't we?"

I said yes, we sure could. Aunt Julep, from what I could tell, was not the stickler for cleaned rooms and made beds that my mother was. In fact, she had never once asked us to do any chores, and her own apartment was the epitome of sloth. She encouraged the licking of mixing bowls and the shirking of bedtimes.

My mother was reading the letter. "It says here it's just for a month. We leave on June 19 and come back July 14. So you won't have to worry about getting them off to school, Julep." She looked at me. "If you and Nellie don't want us to go, we won't."

"Go!" I cried.

"Nellie?" said my father.

Nellie was feeding Puppy her beets under the table. "I don't mind," she said.

My parents taped an alphabetical list of emergency numbers to the refrigerator: dentists, opticians, pediatricians, plumbers, poison control. They taped their itinerary below that, with the phone numbers of all the hotels they would be staying in and the clubs where they'd be playing.

"Don't hesitate to call for anything," said my mother. "I'm sure everything will be fine, but—"

"Of course it will!" said Julep, bundling them out the door with their guitars and luggage.

"Boy, I'm glad they're gone!" I said when they finally were. I wasn't really glad, but I thought that Julep would like it if I said so. "So, maybe we could play a game or something?"

"Yes!" said Julep, as if she hadn't been thinking of that, but now that she was it seemed like a good idea. "And I'll tell you what it's called. It's called Clean Up the Basement."

"I don't like that game," said Nellie.

"I don't think I do, either," I said suspiciously.

"Yes, you do, you just don't know it yet," said Julep, herding us downstairs. She must have been planning on playing this game, because there were bottles of cleaning solution, Windex, mops, pails, and rags all arranged neatly on the cement floor.

"First, we mop," she announced. She produced kerchiefs and tied them on our heads.

"I *hate* this game," said Nellie. "And this thing itches." She pulled off her kerchief.

"Louise, you're in charge while I go to the store," said Julep, heading up the stairs. "We're having a party down here, see, and it has to be clean."

"You hear that?" I shoved a rag at Nellie. "We're having a party."

Julep came back with poster board, magic markers, and glitter paint. She traced some words on the board and instructed me to paint them in.

"Who's Madman Zelooky?" I asked.

"Not *mad*man, *Madam*," said Julep, snatching the board out of my hands. "Madam Zelinsky!" She pointed at herself.

"You don't have to yell!" I said. "Your name *isn't* Madam Zelinsky anyway, so how am I supposed to know?"

Aunt Julep was breathing fast. She put the poster board down and sat down at the card table. "My *real* name is Juliet Fenworth," she said, "which I couldn't pronounce when I was little so that's why I'm Julep now, although a mint julep on a hot afternoon certainly hits the spot."

I nodded, baffled. Julep went on.

"My *stage* name is Madam Zelinsky now, you understand? If I'm Juliet Fenworth, the only reason people will come see me is because they recognize my father's name, and that would be cheating, see?"

"Not really," I admitted.

"Just color it in!" she said, throwing the poster board on the table. "Make it glorious and sparkly."

While I was making the poster board glorious and sparkly and Nellie was giving Puppy a bath in the sink by the washing machine, Julep began making changes of her own upstairs. She moved her things out of the attic apartment and into my parents' bedroom.

"To keep an eye on you two," she told us. She went back to wearing her kimono and left her hair down to froth about her neck and face.

My parents were a big hit on their tour. They called four times the first week and twice the second. The third week they called once, to tell us they'd been extended for another month, and the fourth week they didn't call at all. I wanted to tell them that Julep had taught Nellie to float across the room. Nellie fit into Julep's old sari perfectly.

I wanted to tell my parents about the people who came to our house every Friday and Saturday night—people I'd never seen before in my life. They filed inside and made their way down to the basement and then sat in all the chairs we'd taken from upstairs: green kitchen chairs, leather chairs from my father's study, antique oak chairs from the dining room, the red rocking chair, lawn chairs and fold-out metal chairs. It was too much trouble to bring them all back up again after each performance, so when we weren't in the basement we sat on the floor.

I wanted to tell them how Puppy could twirl in the air and how Nellie could go into a trance and be so still you'd swear she was dead. Julep, cinched up in her red kimono, hair bubbling about her face like some great soufflé (she sprayed it), would wave Dr. Fenworth's wand and hypnotize my sister. Nellie would start to talk in an old man's voice, or a little boy's, or a young woman's, and she would tell how she had fallen off a cliff or been drowned or shot. Nellie herself seemed unfazed by these trances and would come out of them with a yawn and a giggle. She was much better at this sort of thing than I was; the only voice I could produce sounded suspiciously like Donald Duck's. And as for flying, I could only make it halfway across the room before I'd start thinking about how impossible it was and slip out of the air. Aunt Julep said it was impossible for bees to fly, too—they were too heavy for their wings—and that it was a good thing nobody thought to tell the bees. Then she said it was like swimming, except I couldn't swim, either.

Finally, because I simply could not be hypnotized to Julep's satisfaction, she gave me a book called *Secrets of Old-Time Science Experiments* and told me that was more my cup of tea. I pored over the pages and learned how to force an egg into a bottle and make a wine glass dance. Aunt Julep was impressed when I showed her the Electric Broomstick trick and said maybe someday I could do that as an opening act.

But mainly, I was the designated door person. I sat on a stool at the top of the basement steps and collected the dollar admission in my mother's Panama hat. From downstairs, I could hear trumpets and trains and the startled gasps of satisfied customers.

On the Fourth of July, Julep made chocolate cupcakes with red, white, and blue icing and conjured some of our Founding Fathers for a parade in the basement. In a silver-spangled shawl of twilight blue, she led the gauzy forms of George Washington and Thomas Jefferson in a circle around the card table, while Nellie beat time with a tambourine. Julep said not only was it entertaining, it was educational, too. She said she'd come a long way from producing Susan B. Anthony from her ear. Then she started chattering excitedly about the possibility of waging the Revolutionary War right there in basement, complete with musket fire and cannons. But Nellie said blood scared her, and I said if it was anything like the movie *Johnny Tremain*—which I'd been forced to watch about ten times already—then no thanks. I hoped Aunt Julep wouldn't turn sly and try to trick us into learning anything.

But instead of waging any great battles in our basement, she began having private meetings down there during the week. She could—simply by touching an object that had belonged to a departed loved one—provide long-distance service to the Great Beyond. Aunt Julep said that, for the most part, people didn't want to talk to their dear ones for any good reason—like catching them up on things, for instance, or inquiring as to how *they* were doing. "Noo, it's always, 'I broke your favorite vase when I was ten and blamed it on Jimmy, can you ever forgive me?' or 'Didn't I hear you mention once about a stash of loot buried somewhere in the backyard?'" Julep wouldn't tell me the reaction of the spirit world to this type of inquiry, but many customers came flying up the basement steps in such a fit of weeping that they forgot to take their beloved's lace hanky or cameo broach or stopwatch. Julep acquired an extensive collection of these objects.

All this manifesting of parents going on downstairs made me miss my own even more. Lately, whenever I tried to call them, they had just left, and suddenly the list of emergency numbers as well as their itinerary was gone from the refrigerator door.

"What are you talking about?" Julep said when I demanded to know where they were. She and Nellie were sitting on the living room floor, playing cards. "You've always been such an imaginative child! But I suppose it's natural to make things up when you're orphaned so young."

"I'm not making this up!" I yelled. "And I'm not an orphan. My parents are on the road, singing."

"I think," said Julep gently, "that you're just saying this because we watched *The Sound of Music* last night. Go fish."

"That's not why," I said, suddenly unsure. I looked at Nellie. "You remember our parents, don't you?"

"No," she said, without looking up. "They're dead."

Instead of holding down the fort I had let it fly away. Nellie was too young to recognize the impossibility of the situation; like bees, she couldn't appreciate the fact that she wasn't able to fly. But I was old enough to know better. Dogs did not twirl in the air, George Washington and Thomas Jefferson did not manifest beside the washer-dryer, my sister could not fly, and Aunt Julep was not—as she was now claiming—our departed mother's sister. What looked like one thing—a pencil suspended in the air, a bewitched tennis ball—was really something else. I had worked my way back and forth through *The Secrets of Old-Time Science Experiments*, and I thought I knew a few things about illusions.

"Well, if our parents are so dead," I said, "why don't you just poof them up?"

"*Poof* them, dear?" Julep shook her head. "I don't poof, I *invoke*. And I don't think you're aware of how disappointing that kind of thing can be." She wiped her forehead with one of her many lace hankies. "Besides, I don't think I have anything to poof *with*."

"What about this!" I cried, waving my mother's Panama hat. "Where did it come from?"

Aunt Julep picked it up and put it on her head. "From Disney World last year, sweetie. I wore it so I wouldn't burn."

I wasn't entirely convinced that my parents were dead, but what evidence was there, truly, that they had ever lived here? I remembered my mother's perfume, Chanel No. 5, but when I looked in the bathroom cabinets there was nothing but cold cream and Noxzema, and the Russian Red lipstick Aunt Julep wore. I remembered my father's shaving cream and electric razor, but they were gone, too. My parents' dresser drawers—if in fact they had ever belonged to them—were filled with Julep's sweaters and robes. What I remembered as my father's study was now full of books with titles like *The Amazing Tarot* and *Voices from Beyond*. Aunt Julep had printed out fliers on his computer: "Madam Zelinsky, Magic and More." It was the "More" part that worried me.

That night, when I could hear Julep's deep, even breathing coming from my parents' room, I crept down the steps to the basement. I wasn't entirely sure what I planned to do there; how can you break a spell if you don't believe in it? Her tarot cards were stacked neatly at one corner of the card table, and her crystal ball sat in the middle, on a big lace doily. Julep said the crystal ball was like a TV, and some people just had better reception than others. When I looked at it all I could see was my own face, silver and moonlike, as if in the back of a spoon. Julep said she could see the Agonies of Ages in it, and for a moment I thought I knew what she meant.

My stomach rumbled. For dinner Aunt Julep had made Jiffy Pop. We had stood in the kitchen, passing the bag around until it was gone. Initially, this kind of thing had endeared her to me, but I gradually grew tired of what she called Presto Food. She purchased groceries based entirely on their entertainment value: fudge and cookie dip kits; cereal that snapped, crackled, and popped; all manner of gummy creatures; string cheese. Suddenly I wanted to sit at the kitchen table and drink a glass of vanilla milk. I wanted the macaroni and cheese that was stashed back in the cupboard. Then I wanted to go into the living room and sit in the red rocker and watch television. It seemed like a reasonable enough wish and one that didn't require any hocus-pocus to get.

I picked up one of the green kitchen chairs and hauled it as quietly as I could up the steps and then pulled it down the dark hallway to the kitchen. I turned on the light and admired the results of my efforts: the kitchen was beginning to materialize into its former self. In the morning I would bring up the other chairs. I would put everything back the way it was. I tiptoed back down the steps for the red rocker. It was more unwieldy, and instead of picking it up, I knocked it over, into the aluminum utility shelf. From far back in the house I heard Puppy's wild barking and the sharp clicking of his toenails as he raced down the hall and came skittering down the basement steps.

Then came the angry slapping of Aunt Julep's feet. Two pink slippers appeared on the top step under swishing red silk.

"Louise?" she shouted. She slapped down a few more steps and leaned down until I could see the hair puffed around her neck. "What do you think you're *doing*?" she hollered when she could see me. Her face and neck were bright red; her eyebrows puckered into an angry V at the top of her head, reminding me of geese flying south.

I pulled up the rocker and proceeded to haul it to the bottom of the steps.

"I'm going to watch TV," I announced, feeling suddenly ridiculous. "I'm going to drink vanilla milk and watch TV."

Puppy was still prancing around my feet.

"Let go of that chair and take Puppy upstairs." She stamped her foot.

"No," I said and scooped up the dog. He licked me on the chin.

There was silence. Then Aunt Julep began making her way down the stairs. She was gripping the handrail and her red kimono was coming untied, revealing an expanse of pale and lumpy stomach.

"Why are you doing this?" she said and gazed at me mournfully. She tugged her kimono closed. "Don't you want me to teach you how to fly?"

"That's impossible," I told her. "People can't fly, and Susan B. Anthony can't come out your ear, either. It's all made up. It's all a trick."

I stood there with my hands on my hips, challenging her, but she was just a sad old woman and she knew it. I had won.

She gave me a long, level look and then turned around in her pink slippers and made her way up the stairs. Puppy struggled from my arms and ran after her. After a moment, I hauled the rocking chair upstairs and put it where it belonged, in front of the television set.

In the morning, Nellie and Julep and Puppy were gone, and there was a dent in the gravel where the orange Bronco had been. I waited around all day, watching television. I fixed myself macaroni and cheese.

At 6:30, people began showing up to have their fortunes told and talk to the spirits of absent loved ones. I took the sign inside but they kept coming. I turned off the porch light and went down to the basement and sat at the card table, listening to the doorbell. The crystal ball and tarot deck were gone, and the Panama hat was upside down on the table, next to a half-burnt stick of jasmine incense.

I picked up the hat and stared into it. "Hello?" I asked, feeling sad and foolish and strangely hopeful. "Is anybody there?" Then I closed my eyes and listened hard for the answer.

IVY GREEN

1

The plan was to stop at Graceland on the way home, but then Kaitlin looked at the map and saw how close they would be to Tuscumbia and vowed she would never, ever ask for anything again if they could go, and never, ever forgive her heartless parents if they couldn't.

"Where?" said Glen, her father.

"Tuscumbia! Where Helen Keller was born!"

Kaitlin had gone through a phase four years ago when she was eight—learning the manual alphabet, teaching herself some Braille, blindfolding herself and stumbling around the living room—but Meg, her mother, said, "I'm surprised to hear you're still holding a torch for Helen Keller."

"Don't make it sound gross, Mother," Kaitlin said. "You make everything sound gross."

"She carries a torch for *Johnny!*" her ten-year-old brother, Ricky, said. This was either true or not true enough to make Kaitlin fly at him, shrieking and pummeling, and finally Glen said he couldn't take it anymore and slammed out of the room.

When the children had calmed down and were watching Nickelodeon curled up on the bed like puppies, Meg said, "Your father really, really wants to go to Graceland. He's been talking about it since last year."

"El-vis! El-vis!" Ricky chanted, though he had no idea who Elvis was.

"He talks about it *every* year," said Kaitlin, "and every year we decide to skip it. So what's wrong with skipping it again?" She sat up and stared imploringly at her mother. "This is so very, very important to me," she said.

"I know," Meg said, and patted her daughter on the leg. Kaitlin flinched automatically, the way she did when either of her parents touched her, and then something strange happened: she smiled and took her mother's hand.

She's learning how to play us, Meg thought, and felt both uneasy and oddly proud. *She's learning how to get what she wants.*

When the children were asleep, or pretending to be, Meg left the room and went downstairs to the bar where, as usual, Glen was planted on a stool chatting with the bartender, a woman with a fluffy yellow mullet and sad eyes. Meg thought of asking him, "If you like confiding in strangers so much, why didn't you keep going to therapy?" And then he would say, "Because you hated it, too," which was the truth. Therapists were always frowning or making notes or saying, "How do you feel about that?" It was like putting a message in a bottle and flinging it triumphantly into the ocean, only to have it come bobbing back a minute later.

The bartender was dragging on a cigarette and nodding at Glen, who was telling her, "I remember when he was *shot*, you know? Wait, I mean, when he died. He wasn't shot. Who am I thinking of?"

"John Lennon?" the bartender said.

Glen knew Meg was there but was ignoring her. "Right! But when Elvis *died*, that's what I mean. I was on vacation with my parents, at Rehoboth Beach. My dad cried for hours."

"I thought it was your mom who cried for hours," said Meg.

"They both did," Glen said, not looking at her.

"Beer?" said the bartender, blowing smoke in Meg's direction.

"I'll just have some of his," she said, taking a swig from Glen's Coors Light bottle. "You come here often?" she said to him, but he wasn't going for it. They'd done this before, pretended to pick each other up in a Holiday Inn bar while the kids slept upstairs, but it never turned out well. Once, they'd gone back to the room and had furtive, uncomfortable sex in the bathroom, until four-year-old Ricky had nearly walked in on them.

"I want the kids to see Graceland," Glen said. "Maybe we can do both—Elvis and that other place."

"You want yourself to see Graceland," Meg said. "And we can't do both."

Glen was staring at her with drowning eyes. She felt almost sorry for him, for both of them. She'd wanted to see Graceland, too.

"You'll get over it," she said firmly. "There are some things Kaitlin won't ever get over."

He opened his mouth to say something and then—wisely, Meg thought—shut it.

2

The next morning they finally pulled away from damn Cracker Barrel and got back on the road. He was doing the best he could, wasn't he? The kids insisted on eating every breakfast at Cracker Barrel when they were on vacation, and then whined for money to buy some crap in the gift shop. Every morning! Not that he wouldn't miss it, he knew, next summer when he was living alone in some apartment. It would be the first summer in twelve years that he didn't make the trip to Florida to see Meg's parents. Would Meg and the kids go alone? Or would Meg's parents finally visit them for a change? It depressed him, it pissed him off—"Slow *down*, Glen," Meg warned—and it really wasn't his fault at all. He had wanted to work things out.

"There's nothing left to work out," Meg had said wearily, and he knew it was true. This was six months ago, just after Ricky's bicycle accident (a bruised rib, a broken leg) and when their son had recovered and their daughter had stopped threatening to run away from home (because all they cared about was Ricky), and when he found another job after getting laid off, and when Meg finally got her real estate license and they had a little more money rolling in—when, in short, everything was finally looking up—he and Meg looked at each other and realized they hadn't had sex in over a year. And didn't want to.

Then, of course, he had messed things up by kissing that waitress, but his worse sin was confessing to it. He had actually, stupidly, expected Meg to get a little jealous—maybe that would give their relationship some spark again—but instead she just said, "Fine. You can move in with her whenever you want."

They'd tried therapy, but that lasted about four sessions because the therapist was always trying to get them to read books and do trust exercises, which required an effort neither of them could muster.

And then he kissed another waitress, but didn't confess. And did more he didn't confess to. And when he and Meg finally said it out loud two months ago—"Let's get a divorce"—they had desperate, sad, exhilarating sex with each other, and it seemed so final that they both cried afterward.

"Daddy's going to get us all killed," Kaitlin said from the back seat, as he cut off a slow-moving Budweiser truck and earned a honk from its driver. "Just because he doesn't like Helen Keller."

"Hel-en," Ricky chanted softly, sweetly, and Glen felt such a surge of love for his son that his throat closed up and he slowed down to sixty-five miles per hour. Ricky could whine for hours about insignificant things, but he had spent six weeks in a cast with barely a complaint. "It's cool 'cause all my friends will sign it!" he had said, ever optimistic, and sure enough he came home his first day back from school with so many signatures you could hardly see the cast through them. Ricky would be fine. Ricky would adapt. It was Kaitlin they were worried about—so moody, spending so much time in her room. She seemed both younger than her years and older. Her only two friends were sixth graders from ballet class. (She was terrible at ballet—she knew it, too.) She washed her face with prescription soap, but she still had terrible acne. It broke his heart, it did, that his daughter was being so terribly buffeted about by adolescence. But would going to Helen Keller's house really make it any easier when her parents told her they were getting a divorce? He remembered his own parents' divorce, how pissed off he'd been—but he was seventeen, he had friends and a motorcycle. He had Meg, too, by then—high school sweethearts, that old cliché, who grew up and grew apart, another cliché. And what would his children think of him when he told them he was moving in with Rachel, the waitress at the Sizzler they'd been going to for years? When he told them he had fallen in love with her, wanted to marry her for god sakes?

What would *Meg* think? If he was as honest and straightforward as she was, he would have done the right thing and told her about Rachel as soon as he realized things were serious. But he was a coward. Thinking of Rachel he felt aroused and ashamed, and it was all he could do to keep his foot from pushing down harder on the gas.

"Why don't we go to church?" Ricky asked suddenly, as they passed yet another behemoth Baptist edifice. "Didn't we used to go to church?"

"You hated church," Meg said. "We all hated church."

"I liked it," said Kaitlin. "I would still go."

"Well, get one of your friends to take you," Glen said. "Get Debbie, that girl you used to make fun of until she started making fun of you. She liked church."

He had meant to be funny, but it came out mean. Meg gave his hand a warning squeeze and Kaitlin whimpered a little, and he felt like a jerk. Then Ricky started whining about the oldies station they were listening to. "Change it! I hate this song!"

"You've never heard this song," Meg said. "How can you hate it?"

"I hate it!" he shrieked, and clamped his hands over his ears. "Change it!"

"Shut up!" shouted Kaitlin, and kicked her brother. "Just for god sakes shut the hell up!"

Then Meg turned around and said, "Your father *will* pull over," but he wasn't about to pull over. He was speeding up in fact, passing a camper from Missouri toting some other family toward or away from their own vacation. He made eye contact with the father in the driver's seat, a bald man in a sun visor who looked as anxious and confused as he was.

3

The father was trying to pay with a credit card, but they didn't accept credit cards at Ivy Green.

"We just aren't set up for that," Janet explained. "But there's an ATM machine just down the street." She smiled in what she hoped was a sincere-looking way, but she was not in the mood for grumpy families. At church this morning she had prayed for Tolerance, Patience, and a Purpose in Life, which is what she prayed for every week. After church she had felt no different, still edgy and unsettled, but she shook Brother Gregory's hand and said thank you for an inspiring sermon (not that she was paying attention) and even suffered Mavis Wallace's insufferable, prying questions about Brenda, her daughter, not that Brenda was any of Mavis's business. When Janet got home, she decided to test the Lord (which she knew she shouldn't do) to see if he'd answered her prayers and called Brenda in Houston to say hello and ask if she'd given any more thought to making things legal with What's-His-Face.

"Terry," Brenda said. She sighed in a way that sounded suspiciously like the way Janet's husband had sighed for many years, prompting Janet to demand, "Are you smoking a cigarette?" and Brenda to tell her no, of course not, and was Janet calling just to pick on her?

All of which proved to Janet that the Lord had not answered her prayers. And now here she was, donating her time to a Good Cause like she did every Sunday, and she was once again being tested. Because this man, this father, was just standing there glaring at her like she'd insulted him, like she'd said what she was really thinking, which was: *Why do you let your daughter dress like a little harlot?*

"How far away is this ATM?" the mother asked, coming forward and leaning heavily on the countertop. Janet caught a whiff of sour underarm smell.

"Two blocks, that's it. Take a left out of the drive, then a right." She tried to smile, but from the corner of her eye she was aware that the little boy had wandered into the sitting-room-turned-museum across the hall and was getting his dirty fingers all over Helen Keller's Braille typewriter.

"Why don't we just go home," the boy moaned and struck his head against a glass case, prompting the little girl in the too-short shorts to grab him by the shirt and say, "Cut it *out*. Behave yourself for once." So maybe she wasn't as untamed as she looked.

"There's no point in all of us going," the father said. "You all stay here, and I'll be right back."

"We'll hold the tour," Janet said, but the father just waved his hand as he disappeared down the hall and slammed out the screen door.

"He doesn't care about the tour," the mother said. "You might as well just give it to us." She crossed her arms, as if issuing a dare. The boy darted out of the room and clattered up the steps, perhaps to wreak havoc in the roped-off bedrooms.

Yes, Janet thought—this was a test. But then the little girl stepped forward and said, very politely, "Is this Helen Keller's actual dining room?" and Janet said yes, and not only that, these were the actual dishes she didn't manage to break!

"Helen Keller *ate* off those," the girl said to her mother.

"The whole Keller family," Janet added. "And of course Miss Sullivan, too. It's quite remarkable, the history that happened here."

"Kaitlin taught herself Braille, didn't you?" the girl's mother said, smiling at her daughter. The girl mumbled something and shrugged, shyly. She reminded Janet a little bit of Brenda, before Brenda lost her way. That's how Brother Gregory phrased it, and at first Janet had thought he meant literally, because Brenda was blind, and she had bristled and said, "No, she's got a seeing eye dog and an excellent sense of direction."

The tour didn't take long—dining room, sitting room, downstairs bedroom, upstairs bedrooms—and after they all followed her dutifully down the steps back to the front hallway, Janet said, "Feel free to browse the museum and roam the grounds. The cottage is just to the right out the back door, and the pump is there, too."

"The pump!" the girl shrieked, and flew out the door, her brother in pursuit.

"They've been cramped up in the car all day," the mother said. "I should get souvenirs. But you only take cash, right? Which we don't have."

"Your husband's been gone a bit," Janet ventured. "Hope he didn't get lost."

"Oh, he's lost all right," the mother said and gave a bitter laugh. "Don't worry, he'll be back eventually. It's not like we can leave if he isn't."

Then she just stood there, scrutinizing an Ivy Green coffee mug, so Janet said, "You have a lovely family. Whereabouts are you from?"

"What about her mother?"

Janet didn't like it when someone ignored a simple question by asking an unrelated question. It was something Brenda did more and more often. For instance, when Janet—unable to help herself—finally said, "*When* are you going to get married?" ashamed that it came out like a desperate whine, Brenda gave one of her smoky sighs and said, "So how's the weather in Alabama?"

The mother put the coffee mug back on the counter, just a little too harshly, and picked up a souvenir pencil. "Helen's mother," she said. "You told us about her father and about Annie and even about the slaves."

"Servants," Janet corrected.

"But what about her mother?"

"Oh, Mrs. Keller was a Memphis belle!" Janet said, feeling suddenly invigorated. Why did no one ever ask about Mrs. Keller? Why did no one care about her? "And what an interesting story— she was twenty years Captain Keller's junior, practically the same age as his oldest son! They didn't get along a-tall," she added.

"And there were times when she and the Captain didn't speak for *weeks*." She was immensely pleased with herself for having dredged up this information.

"Poor thing," the mother said. "How awful was it for her, to have a daughter like that?"

Janet wasn't quite sure what she was hearing. "All children are a blessing," she said sharply. "Mrs. Keller loved her family, and Helen Keller did a lot of good in the world." Obviously! Then, because the woman was staring at her in a very strange way, Janet said kindly, "I just know your husband will be back any minute now."

The mother snapped her head up as if Janet had said something terrible. Her eyes were bloodshot. "I can't tell anyone this," she said, in a choking voice.

"Oh, no, please—" Janet looked hopefully toward the front door, but there were no cars in the parking lot, no one coming to rescue her from whatever the Lord was about to test her with.

"I can't even tell my own husband I'm pregnant—because I don't *want* it." The woman was twisting the pencil in her hands. "And it *is* his, if that's what you're wondering." She glared at Janet as if she'd been challenged.

Janet, who had not been wondering any such thing, was imagining Brenda saying to her, "Oh, lighten up for god sakes," the way she sometimes did, but it was impossible, she couldn't lighten up. "Is the child—damaged?" she ventured, barely able to speak. "Because my own—"

"Who knows?" the mother interrupted. Then she gave a sharp laugh. "Who isn't?"

The sun was too bright, too hot, glaring through the window, but Janet couldn't move.

"So he never has to know, does he?" The mother was breathing fast, nearly panting; outside, her children were running in circles around the servant's quarters. "No one has to know."

Janet could feel her body turning cold now, marbleizing like the bust of Helen Keller in the next room, big blank eyes staring kindly at nothing. She wanted to say: *I* know. I am not *no one*, but then—at last, too late—came the sound of footsteps on the porch: the porch where Janet always imagined the child-Helen fuming in dark silence, waiting for someone to finally make contact.

4

Standing at the famous pump where Annie had wrestled Helen to the ground and spelled into her hand (they had seen *The Miracle Worker* during third grade assembly), Kaitlin felt calm and wise. She was no idiot. She knew her parents were getting a divorce. They didn't exactly argue quietly, and her bedroom was right next door to theirs. She had heard them use words with each other that, said in a quieter tone of voice, might have led to the muffled shuffling that always made her turn on her iPod. But these words, in a different tone of voice, made someone (her father?) slam out the door and down the hallway. Every night after that, they had tucked her and Ricky into bed, gone to their own room, and then someone had tiptoed down the hall to spend the night on the sofa.

She had been waiting for them to announce the family vacation was off; they weren't going to drive to Florida to see the grandparents after all. But this didn't happen, and not only did they take the trip, her parents had faked being happy. They spent the night together in her mother's childhood bedroom, just like always; they took Kaitlin and Ricky to Disney World and all got sunburned, as usual. They bought Ricky everything he asked for and tried to ply Kaitlin with presents as well. "Don't you think I'm too old for that?" she said, rebuffing her mother's attempts to buy her a stuffed Dumbo. She actually wouldn't have minded going to Graceland.

Now, armed with information about the state of their family, she felt herself looking down on her brother as if from a distance; he was an innocent child, and she was closing in on adulthood at a pace that made her dizzy. At first it seemed as if womanhood would be all nastiness and deceit: smells and hairs and hiding the Tampax box under her bed so her mother wouldn't find it and sit her down to tell her (again) all the things she already knew and didn't want to think about. When she was eleven, Kaitlin's mother had actually produced a condom from a square baby-blue packet and held it limply in front of her, at which point Kaitlin had stomped off to her room and slammed the door. "I'm just trying to make sure you're informed," her mother called after her. "You shouldn't be embarrassed!"

"Yes, you should," said her friend Debbie. Or her ex-friend. Six weeks ago, before school let out, Debbie had informed John Masterson that the love letters he kept finding stuffed in his locker were from Kaitlin—a lie Kaitlin couldn't bring herself to refute because that would mean actually speaking to John, a ninth grader whose gaze made Kaitlin feel full of static and fuzz, like a balloon did when you rubbed it on your sweater and it made your arm hairs stand up. Debbie herself was the writer of those love letters, and it was only because Kaitlin insisted on correcting her spelling

("You're spelling *soul mate* as if he's a fish.") that Debbie took her revenge. It had all seemed like the worst thing that could ever happen, and for a few hours Kaitlin had even considered running away or jumping off the top bleacher at the track. She had written out her own long letter to John, saying good-bye, then folded it in her algebra book where Ricky found it and started reading it out loud to himself before Kaitlin had a chance to tear it up and punch him in the head.

But now, a quote from somewhere (a movie?) kept rolling around in her head, something about with great power comes great responsibility. That night in the motel room after her parents had agreed to go to Ivy Green instead of Elvis's house, the implications of this newfound power had thrilled her so much she could hardly fall asleep. She didn't even care about Helen Keller; she just wanted to see if she could make her parents change their plans. She wanted, it was true, to punish them—not so much for getting a divorce, though certainly for that, too—but mainly for keeping it a secret. For thinking she was too stupid to figure it out.

She would show them who was stupid.

And actually, now that they were here, she was glad they'd come. A bit of her eight-year-old self had emerged as they pulled into the driveway, and even more when they were actually inside Helen Keller's house, looking at the things Helen had never been able to see.

The pump was small and shiny black, enclosed by a tiny white fence. Kaitlin closed her eyes for a moment, and when she opened them the world seemed new. She walked back to the house thinking that her parents were good people, feeling ashamed for what she had almost done this morning at Cracker Barrel: stood up and announced loudly, "I know you're getting a divorce, so you might as well admit it!" She'd liked the idea of all the other customers staring at her, at them, their forks dangling over their blueberry pancakes.

Her mother was out on the porch, squinting into the sun setting behind the iron gates. Ricky ran around in circles, pretending to be an airplane. Kaitlin paused for a moment in front of the dining room table, the scene of so much fighting and dish smashing. Her father was finally paying their admission fees—he looked so old, so weary and distracted. Then the elderly woman looked up and saw Kaitlin and said, "Little girl, do you really know Braille?"

"I did. A little," Kaitlin admitted. She felt morbidly shy, acutely aware of her un-Helen-Keller-like acne.

"Would you like to see something?" the woman asked, and removed her bulk from behind the counter. "Here in the museum?"

Kaitlin was about to say they were getting ready to leave, but her father said gruffly, "We'll wait," and gave a little wave on his way down the hall.

The museum was once a sitting room, but now it was filled with glass cases and plaques and photographs. For some reason, rows and rows of books with Japanese script lined the shelves. Kaitlin followed the woman to a desk, where an ancient contraption sat beside an equally ancient-looking placard: HELEN KELLER'S BRAILLE TYPEWRITER. "I shouldn't do this," the old lady said, rolling a piece of paper into the thing. "This is strictly forbidden." She was trembling a little. "But I don't think Helen would mind, do you?"

"No," said Kaitlin, because she didn't. She watched the old woman type surprisingly quickly—so fast, in fact, that she wondered if she was typing anything at all, or just playing.

"Here," the woman said, ripping the paper out of the machine and handing it to Kaitlin. She really was trembling now, and she gripped Kaitlin around the wrist with her dry old fingers. "This is for you."

Kaitlin stared at the raised dots. "I can't read this."

"When you get home," the old woman said. "You can figure it out, and then you'll know what to do."

"About what?" Kaitlin asked, but then her father honked the horn, something he did when he was in a particularly bad mood.

"Good-bye," the old woman said firmly. "We're closing now."

Outside again, Kaitlin stood on the porch of Ivy Green and looked at her family—her father craning out the driver's window like an angry cuckoo; her mother leaning against the car with her arms crossed, staring at her shoes. Ricky was still running in crazed circles around a towering maple—a tree Helen Keller must have touched before and after the secrets of the world were unlocked to her. Kaitlin folded the Braille paper carefully in half—a souvenir of their last family trip, a message just for her—then put it in her purse and ran to the car.

CRUMBS

The smell hits me when we're in her yard—the yard that used to be mine, too—and I get that familiar, doomed feeling in my stomach, and it's everything I can do not to run for my life.

"You okay, Dad?" Kyle asks me, and I nod and grab his hand. He's eight, the same age I was when everything happened. He doesn't know about all that. He knows I don't talk about my childhood, and that I haven't seen my sister in seven years. He knows I can't bear the smell of fresh-baked cookies and cakes.

Lisa knows it too, which is why I'm frankly surprised that she chose to make gingerbread on the one day we agreed to be civil to each other, for Kyle's sake, and at least try to act like a family.

I'm sweating by the time we get to the door, which Lisa pulls open before I can knock. She looks slim and beautiful; she's wearing a red velvet dress that grazes her knees. She takes the bowl of hummus Kyle is carrying and sniffs it skeptically.

"I helped Dad make it," Kyle tells her, and she gives me a dark look. I'm holding a tray of raw vegetables—squash, cucumber, carrots, radishes—and she pointedly ignores me and marches toward the kitchen, Kyle trailing behind her.

Her boyfriend, Bob, is sitting on the sofa in the living room, wearing that ridiculous crown because God forbid anyone should forget he's a prince. He raises his eyebrows at me and presses his lips together. This, I suppose, is his way of saying hello. His ermine cape is draped over the back of the couch.

"I thought this was supposed to be family," I say to him. "Screwing my ex-wife does not make you family."

"Lisa wanted me here," he tells me, and fiddles with his crown self-consciously. And he should feel self-conscious, the little prick. I feel certain that she met him before we were divorced. She must have found him down at the pond behind the elementary school. I can imagine her, scooping up frogs frantically, putting her lips to them, wishing for someone—anyone—to take her away from the life we'd made together.

Or maybe he was somebody's cast-off, conjured into existence by a high school girl desperate for a prom date. And once the prom was over, she left him for someone age appropriate, someone with a cool car who likes hip-hop.

In the kitchen I say, "I can't believe you invited him!" I feel woozy from the cookie fumes. "And baking that stuff. My God, Lisa, you know what that does to me." My eyes are stinging.

"Oh, lay off," she says. "It's Christmas. We can't eat raw carrots for Christmas."

"I brought more than raw carrots. I brought squash, too. And radishes."

"Kyle honey," she says, "go take the gingersnaps out to the living room while I talk with your father."

Kyle casts me an anxious look. "It's okay, kiddo," I tell him.

When he's disappeared through the swinging kitchen door, I say, "What are you trying to do to me?"

"Nothing," she says. "This is what normal families *do*."

I think of reminding her that all she knows about families is what she's seen on television; that if she came from a normal family of her own she wouldn't have ended up stashed in the basement of the university's history department for a century. I think of telling her that if she's going to bring up my past, I can bring up hers.

But I don't, because I love our son and I don't want him to hear us arguing. He's heard enough of that in his life.

The kitchen is a mess of mixing bowls and batter; there are raisins and chocolate chips strewn across the counter. When we were married, when we loved each other, she wouldn't even watch cooking shows on TV. We ordered Chinese take-out and made vegetarian lasagna together—I have no problems with lasagna—and spaghetti without meatballs.

Once, when we were first dating, she ordered a steak at Bennigan's and when she saw me go pale she asked what the matter was. I just shook my head. Still, she changed her order to a veggie quesadilla. It wasn't until the night before our wedding that I could bring myself to tell her what had happened, how the smell of burnt flesh had followed me and my sister for miles through the forest.

"At least you have the decency not to cook meat," is what I say to her now. It's meant to be a peace offering, a kind of thank-you, but I know that's not how it comes out. She pulls the oven open and the smell of gingerbread fills the kitchen.

"Goddamn you," I say, under my breath. I head down the hall to the bathroom and hold myself up against the counter until I can stop shaking.

"Your past," she said to me once, "is what made you the man I fell in love with."

But she had been sleeping for a hundred years when I met her; all she could remember were her dreams. She had been watching soap operas to catch up on modern society.

A graduate student at the university had found her in the basement of the history department; she was spread out across a row of dusty file boxes. At first, he thought she was a grad assistant taking a nap, but then he got closer and saw the dust on her, and the damask gown, and the tendrils of hair coiling down to the hard floor. He kissed her—he was gay, but he hated to see somebody so pretty covered in dust—and for a while they were roommates until she got a job as a receptionist at National Semiconductor Corporation.

That's where she met me. We ate lunch together in the conference room—she thought it was funny that I brought peanut butter and jelly—and told each other about our lives, a little at a time, presenting ourselves in our best light, careful not to scare the other one off.

I didn't care that she couldn't remember her childhood, and she didn't care that I remembered mine too well.

It all happened much too fast, the way these things sometimes do.

A few months after we were married, she started saying things like, "I wish Brent had never woken me up," and once she moved out to stay on his sofa for a few days. She was tired of my vegan diet; she was tired of my sister calling at all hours to tell me our father was ill. She was tired of waking up in the middle of the night to find me standing in the yard in my pajamas. Once, I made it halfway down the street.

In the soap operas she taped on the VCR, the men ate steak and rescued women from atop windy cliffs and killed bad guys with their bare hands. Sometimes they came back from the dead. They never cried in their sleep.

Sometimes I pretended to sleepwalk when I was really awake.

And then she got pregnant with Kyle. She turned off the soap operas and instead read books about what to expect when you're expecting.

When Kyle was born, we held our breath, waiting for an old woman with a curse, or an old man with a spindle, a queen with a grudge. But no one came.

When I go back out to the living room, Kyle is sitting on the floor, eating cookies, and Bob is pretending to be interested in the train cartoon playing on the VCR.

"Did you tell Bob about the fort?" I ask Kyle, and ease down next to him on the floor.

"You built a fort?" Bob asks politely as he uncrosses then recrosses his chubby legs in their purple velvet pants.

Kyle nods happily. "We just started. We went to Home Depot, didn't we, Dad?"

"You bet we did."

I'd like to see Bob try to build a fort. He'd probably get his cape stuck on a nail. The fort was Kyle's birthday present last week. I wanted to give him something we could do together, something he could be proud of. Something he'd always remember.

"Little snowy for fort-building, isn't it?" Bob asks.

"We probably won't get much done until spring," I tell him, annoyed. "But we bought a tarp. We'll work on it when it's not too cold outside. Then Kyle'll have all the neighborhood kids over to play."

Kyle doesn't say anything to this. He doesn't have many friends. Actually, I'm not sure he has any. He's a quiet kid, like I was. I'm hoping when we get this thing built, he'll be more popular.

Lisa swings into the living room, her skirt swishing, her face flushed from the heat of the kitchen. She sinks onto the sofa next to Bob, gives him a kiss on the cheek.

"If you kiss him on the mouth," I say, "will he turn back into a toad?"

She ignores this. Instead she announces, as if she's just remembered it, "We got a card from your sister. Isn't that nice?"

"Where's the card?" I want to know, and Lisa shrugs.

Of course she's lying about that card, but why?

My sister is a professor of social psychology in Toronto. She has met Kyle exactly once, when he was one, at our father's funeral. Our father had been living with my sister—she took him in when he got ill—and she never forgave me for not helping out more.

"I have a family," I told her. "I can't."

"Don't forget who saved you," she said to me then. "Don't forget who set you free."

She blames me for the bread crumbs. For not being smart enough to figure out what would happen. She hasn't come out and said this, but it's the truth, and it's right there in her eyes, which is why I can't see her again.

"This is nice," I say now. "Are we just going to hang out and watch cartoons? I'm fine with that." I'm aware that my voice is too loud. I grab a carrot. "You should have told me Bob was going to be here; I'd've invited my girlfriend."

Lisa raises her eyebrows at me, and Kyle turns around and says, "Melinda?" and smiles. He loves Melinda. She's technically his babysitter, but we've been sort of seeing each other. She's twenty, and she thinks it's cool that I only eat raw vegetables. She's really into acupuncture, which isn't my thing, but she's sweet, and she doesn't ask me too many questions.

"*Melinda*?" says Lisa. She remembers Melinda from when she first started babysitting, when she was about thirteen. "You've got to be kidding me. But fine. Call her up. The more the merrier."

Before Melinda, I'd been seeing a woman from work for a few weeks, an engineer named Evelyn who was sexy as hell and didn't seem to know it. She knew all about what had happened with Lisa—Lisa, thank God, was no longer working there—and she asked me out for drinks one night. We went out a couple of times, and she told me about her divorce and I told her very little about mine.

The first time I introduced her to Kyle, something flashed across her face, a coldness I'd never seen in her before. Later, when I accused her of this, she cried and said she loved children, that I was imagining things. And maybe I was.

But what if I wasn't?

I know what can happen to a good man when he falls in love with the wrong woman. I tell myself that I'm nothing like my father, that I would never let a woman turn me against my own child. Things were different for me and my sister. Our father was a poor woodcutter, not an electrical engineer. There was a famine. He married Ilsa after he'd been a widower for seven years. She pretended to like us at first.

My sister thinks that anyone can be pushed to make the wrong decisions, under certain social structures and circumstances. She proves this over and over in her lab experiments. Mild-mannered college students will give each other painful electrical shocks; blue-eyed students will bully brown-eyed students; when given the chance, the brown-eyed students will bully the blue-eyeds. And so on.

Melinda is happy to hear from me. "I'm just sitting here watching television," she says. "I'd love to come over. Are you sure it's okay with Lisa?"

"Of course it is," I tell her. "Lisa's boyfriend is here. We're all one big happy family."

"Really?" She sounds doubtful.

I'm in the dining room, talking on my cell phone. In the other room, Lisa and Bob are laughing up a storm, and I suddenly understand what Lisa's up to, with the baking, and mentioning my sister, and having Bob here. She hopes I'll lose it—start crying, perhaps, or throw a vase across the room, or put my fist through the wall, the way I did on our last anniversary when she told me she was leaving. She wants a witness, someone to stand up in court and say I'm an unfit father. She wants full custody. And that's not going to happen.

When I go back to the living room, both Lisa and Bob are looking at me strangely. Kyle is gone. Lisa stands up, as if to make some kind of announcement, but she just stares at me.

"What?" I say. "What's going on? Where's Kyle?"

"I sent him into the kitchen to ice the cupcakes," she says. And then, "Bob says you and Kyle are building a fort."

"Yeah, we are."

"Out of wood? With nails? Tell me about this fort. Tell me what it looks like." She puts her hands on her hips. "Tell me."

You think that if you get away from the worst thing you can imagine, that once you fight for your life and win, you deserve to be happy. And maybe you do, but it doesn't necessarily work that way.

While Lisa stares at me, her face pale, I tell her about the carefully spaced wooden slats, and about the dirt floor. I tell her about the four-foot-high roof.

"And the door?" she says. "The door that locks."

I nod. It hadn't occurred to me to wonder why a little boy would need a padlock on his fort, or why the slats had to be just big enough for a child to poke his finger through.

I slam out the back door and don't stop running until I'm in the foggy woods behind the house. The air is thick and heavy and cold in my chest. The tire swing—which I made for Kyle two years ago—is covered in a layer of ice; the yellow rope is frayed and I remind myself to replace it so it won't break off when Kyle is in midflight.

When I showed Kyle the plans I'd drawn up for the fort, the intricate connection of slats and beams, he had grinned at me with such utter joy that I wanted to get started immediately, weather be damned. "By the spring," I told him, "it'll be done. All the other kids'll want to come over and play with you."

Yesterday, when I was looking for Christmas presents in Wal-Mart, I ended up in the hardware section. I bought a padlock and a chain. I didn't wonder why I needed them.

There's the foggy yellow glow and muted hush of a car moving slowly up the road. After a moment, I recognize Melinda's Corvette. I jog farther into the trees, running until I begin to sweat and the new snow falling from the sky burns against my face. When I stop, I can barely see the glow of the house through the trees.

Somewhere, snow thuds from a branch and the frozen earth shudders. But this is no ancient forest. In a hundred yards I'll be in the parking lot of a Rite Aid. I can't vanish into the wilderness this time. Even if I stand here for an hour, even if I watch the snow fill up my footprints until there's no sign of them at all, there is no way for me to be more lost than I already am.

LET YOURSELF GO

If she gets up and leaves, Martha wonders, just stands up and goes out the door, will Larry follow her? Getting to the door would mean moving back the coffee table and stepping around Larry, then around Walter Morgan, then around Walter's girlfriend, Shelley. And she can't just *leave*—her coat is somewhere down the hall; she would have to ask Dierdre to find it for her, she would have to think of some gracious and apologetic excuse. She can't say, "I've got to get up early for my biopsy"—which isn't even true, it's next week, and which she can't imagine saying anyway. "Are you having fun over there?" Shelley asks, leaning around Larry and smiling crookedly, and Martha says yes, she's having a ball.

Martha doesn't know any of these people, except for Larry, her husband. Walter and Shelley are driving from Connecticut to California, and they've stopped off in Tucson so Shelley can visit her high school friends and Walter can visit Larry. They went to college together in Connecticut until Walter dropped out to go to bartending school. Walter keeps saying he's never been west of the Mississippi but it's crazy what love will make you do. He and Shelley had never even seen each other face to face until she flew east for Christmas two weeks ago, and now he's moving to Los Angeles to be with her. They'd met on the Internet, which always makes Martha think of a great big mesh hammock where you roll around for a while, electronically speaking, until you meet somebody you like.

"You can just get to know a person like you can't when you're face to face," Shelley had told her earlier in the evening. "You can totally be yourself."

"You can meet some weirdos though, can't you?" said Martha, trying hard to think of something, anything to say. She was drinking wine fast, to induce chattiness, but it was just making her tired. "Hook up with some crazy guy and suddenly he's sending you a hundred messages a day and your computer's all *beep-beep-beep*, all day long? Doesn't that happen?"

Shelley supposed it did, she didn't know personally.

Martha sets her plate of lasagna on the glass coffee table and sinks back in her chair, feeling sleepy and small. She closes her eyes briefly and sees an image of a tomato, dangling fatly from a vine. When she thinks of the thing inside her she doesn't think of *cells*—a diagram from her high school biology book—but of vegetables, her childhood terror of swallowing some seed that will take root and grow twining around her insides.

Yesterday, Dr. Hannah Wang had said, "You need a biopsy." Dr. Wang had all the pictures on her desk facing out, so Martha could see her at Disney World with a serious-looking man, both of them wearing Mickey Mouse hats. In another picture, she and the man were standing on top of what looked like a cliff, saddled down with camping gear. Then Dr. Wang said, "The cells are probably *pre*cancerous," and just hearing the word made Martha start to cry. For some reason, the picture of Dr. Wang in the mouse ears made it hard to stop. After that, all Martha felt was tired, too tired to tell Larry or call her mother or take her socks off before going to bed.

With effort, she is able to isolate some of the conversations going on around her. Larry and Walter are talking about friends they knew in Connecticut, people with names like Bob Nauseous and Super Dave and the Tim Man. The women are talking about the toys they played with as children.

"We did the most awful things to Barbie," says a woman in a maroon velvet dress whose name Martha forgot immediately upon being introduced to her. "Our favorite was Ski Accident Barbie. We'd papier-mâché her, like a giant body cast."

"We sold gerbil chews by the side of the road," says Dierdre ("*Dear*-dree," she'd corrected Martha kindly. "With an *r*.") "You know those toilet paper rolls you put in their cages? After they'd chewed them for a while, we'd take them out and paint them— turn them into queens and trains and things." Martha used to try to sell rocks from her driveway. She would set up a card table in front of her house that said "Genuine Arrowheads, 10 for 5 cents." But she doesn't have the energy to yell this across the room; she doesn't like the thought of her voice floating around up there with the other ones, like a kite tangled up and ripped apart in the wind.

This is Dierdre's house; her husband took the carpet and the Nordic Track and the beanbag chair when he moved out. "But he left his CDs and the stereo!" Dierdre said. "And the cats.

Anybody want two cats?" Walter and Shelley are staying with her, sleeping on the futon sofa where the cats, Pipper and Noggin, are dozing side by side above the head of an elfish-looking man in a red tie. Martha is fairly certain his name is Mickey. Mickey's lips are pressed together like a ribbon, but he looks happy, smiling and nodding his head at nothing in particular.

The only other man there is Dierdre's boyfriend, a beautiful, morose Italian in a black turtleneck. He's sitting on the shiny hard floor, leaning against the radiator as if suctioned there. Dierdre told everyone that he has a show in Phoenix next month, and the Italian had nodded solemnly and examined his fingernails and not said a word. Now, he seems to be staring at the wall behind Dierdre's head, as if envisioning some nude portrait of her he'd like to paint there. There are some of his paintings in the bedroom—Martha had accidentally wandered in, looking for the bathroom—and they're all of Dierdre, naked and smudgy and smiling.

Mickey's wife, the largest and loudest of the women, suddenly shouts, "Brigadoon!" and all the other women scream with laughter, rocking back and forth.

"You girls," says Walter. "With your private jokes. You didn't understand that, did you, Martha? It wasn't just some woman thing, was it?"

"Like a weird allusion to menstruation or something?" says Martha, then wishes she hadn't. "No," she says quickly. "I didn't get it." She sits up straighter and smiles. If someone were peering into the window right now, they would think she was entirely calm and at ease. They would see young, healthy people engaged in exuberant conversations. They wouldn't know that Martha is gripping her napkin so hard she has fingernail marks in her palm, or that Larry—who wanted her to be here so badly, who pleaded with her to come—has barely said two words to her all night. They would just see happy people and pristine hardwood floors, forest-green throw rugs, bottles of wine, and stacks of dirty lasagna dishes—which Dierdre is now picking up and carrying to the kitchen.

It's like a commercial for something, a layout in one of those how-to-entertain magazines. A full-color spread, taking up facing pages. For recipes, see page 196. The Christmas tree is twinkling, Frank Sinatra is crooning. Post-holiday spirit, thinks Martha dismally. Tra-la-la.

"I hope no one has any nut allergies," Dierdre calls from the kitchen. "'Cause dessert is pecan pie."

"I think we're all feeling nutty," Shelley says.

"Hey, what'd you think of the lasagna?" says Larry, reaching over and tugging Martha's sleeve. "Everybody, Martha's a food critic."

"You are!" Dierdre shrieks. "Oh my God. Don't even tell me what you thought. I don't even want to know."

"It was wonderful," says Martha, and pinches Larry's forearm hard. "The spices jumped around in my mouth like . . . like. . . Oh, I don't know." She takes a breath. From the corner of her eye, she can see the Italian watching her.

"Words fail her," says Larry, and that's when Martha knows what she's going to say next, feels it already forming, swirling up inside her.

"That sounds so fun." Shelley tilts her head drunkenly at Martha. "Are you a gourmet cook, too?"

"I'm not," Martha says. "I wish I was. Right after the operation I'm going to take classes." She feels suddenly giddy, having said this. She has no intention of taking cooking classes. She wonders briefly if she's going to laugh, but the room has become suddenly, reverently quiet.

"Operation?" says Dierdre politely, returning with four carefully balanced plates of pie, setting them around the table like the petals of some weird, crusty flower.

Martha can feel Larry staring at her. "I've got this thing." She gestures vaguely toward her lower midsection. "This thing that needs to be removed. *Pre*cancerous, definitely."

"What thing?" says Larry, leaning toward her, looking at her abdomen as if he has X-ray vision. "What sort of operation?"

She's aware of everyone's eyes on him, on them, wondering: How could he not know? Why didn't he know? Larry looks stricken; a piece of pie has fallen from his fork to his shirt and clings to one white button. "Laser surgery," she says gently, "the latest technology." Dr. Wang had mentioned something about lasers, but Martha can't remember what. She had said it probably wouldn't be necessary, and had used the words "freezing" and "scraping," as if the cells were Arctic relics that needed excavating. But Martha thinks lasers sound more serious. "And even if I *don't* get the operation, if I did nothing at all, I'd still have ten years to live." She smiles bravely. "So it's not like it's any big deal. I have to use the little food critic's room." She stands. "Dish me up some of that pie," she says to Dierdre on her way down the hall.

The bathroom is a fuzzy, salmon pink, decorated in seashell motif. There's a seashell-shaped plastic pillow in the tub, the soaps are all seashells, the bathmat is a seashell. So is the toilet cover.

Earlier, Martha had marveled at the kind of planning and initiative that went into such coordination. What did the ex-husband think of it? He'd left his electric razor behind; Martha had seen it in the cabinet under the sink. She doesn't look in people's medicine cabinets, but she does look under sinks. There's a half-empty bottle of Grecian Formula down there, too.

Martha can hear whispering in the next room, and she feels a shiver of glee. She'd actually been meaning to tell Larry about the biopsy this morning. She'd wanted to tell him at breakfast, casually, over coffee. She'd wanted to touch his arm and say, "I'll be fine. Don't worry." But that morning, before the alarm even went off, Larry had said, "You know, honey, you're sort of letting yourself go," and she couldn't do it. It seemed suddenly like it was all her fault somehow, as if her body's insides were manifesting an outward slovenliness.

Her first thought was: It's still dark, how can he tell? But then she realized that he meant in general; he meant that as an everyday rule, she was letting herself go.

"What are you talking about?" she'd said, sitting up. "You mean because I wear a dumpy old nightshirt instead of Victoria's Secret? Because I sleep in my socks?"

"No," said Larry, rolling onto his back. He rubbed his eyes. "I don't know," he said. "You just don't seem as well put together as you used to be. Ah. Never mind."

He'd been after her to cut her hair short and dye it red, was that what he meant? Which she wasn't about to do; who knew what that stuff did to your scalp. Besides, she hadn't realized that she had to *be* "well put together"—she was happy that she could be her sloppy self and still be loved. She *liked* that she didn't care if Larry saw her without her makeup, or knew that her underwear was ripped, or saw her eating bean with bacon soup out of the can with a fork. Wasn't that what love was all about? She certainly didn't care if he put the toilet paper roll on backward, or left his socks in the living room, or farted in his sleep—which perhaps he didn't know and which she didn't, even now, have the heart to tell him.

Soon after they'd gotten married, two years ago, she overheard him telling someone, "She crashed right into my life. She slammed her shopping cart right into me, trying to pick me up." This was an outright lie. She was in the checkout at Safeway and suddenly he was there behind her with his red basket (neither of them even had a cart!) calling her Marty Pants—her sixth grade nickname—and saying, "Do you remember me? Larry Griggs?" She didn't, not at first, but she gave him her phone number anyway.

Later, he asked her if she would have gone out with him if he'd just been some random guy in the checkout line, and she said no, she probably wouldn't have.

"Just because I was in your sixth grade class, who says I'm not a psychopath? Who says I haven't been stalking you for the past fifteen years?" This was after three months, and she knew he wasn't a psychopath. She was already in love with him and was trying to think of a way to say this without actually saying it, so she'd told him how amazing it was he'd recognized her that day, how wonderful it was that things could happen to you when you're not even looking.

"Have you been stalking me for fifteen years?" she said. "I hope so."

A year later they were married and he was telling people she slammed into him with her shopping cart. At the time she'd thought it was sort of sweet, in a metaphorical way, but now she considered the possibility that he'd been craving something more interesting and dramatic from the very beginning—some hot-blooded high-heeled girl hunting him down in the Safeway, with a cart of exotic cheeses and wines.

The alarm went off and Larry leaned over her and swatted at it until it fell off the nightstand.

"You want me to lift weights or something, is that it? You want me to be all firm and muscly?" She was shouting now. The alarm clock was still buzzing on the floor and she got out of bed and stepped on it. "I hate to tell you this," she said, "but I've always been this way, it's not a deterioration at all. Maybe it's just finally sunk in that I'm not going to turn into somebody *else*."

"I don't know why I said anything," Larry said. His left arm was slung over his head and his stomach, a little roll of a belly that Martha actually finds endearing, was rising and falling tiredly. "I mean, I'm no Ashton Kutcher."

"See?" she cried. "I don't care that you watch stupid shows with Ashton Kutcher, why can't I eat soup from the can?"

Larry pulled himself out of the covers and looked at her. His eyebrows were the dark, bushy kind that made him always look slightly concerned, so she couldn't tell if he actually was or not. "Calm down," he said. He crawled toward her on his knees, bunching up the covers as he went. "I don't want to fight," he said and wrapped his arms around her waist.

They'd never had a fight, not once, nothing even approximating a fight. It made them feel superior to their more tempestuous friends, who were always screaming at each other and breaking up and getting back together.

"The thing I like most about you," Larry told her once, "is that you're calm yet exciting. You're predictable but spontaneous."

No one had ever described Martha in these terms. Other boyfriends had accused her of being flighty and self-absorbed. This was when they were breaking up. When they were not breaking up, they still said she was flighty and self-absorbed, but they said it kindly. She'd gotten into fights with them, the yelling and screaming kind, but something about Larry made her resist this. She loved him because he made her feel calm and exciting, predictable and spontaneous. (But wouldn't it be better to be one or the other? she wonders now. Instead of all these things that cancel each other out?)

"I'm sorry," she said. "Maybe your second wife will wear Victoria's Secret."

He mumbled something into her bare stomach and she kissed the top of his head.

This was a joke Martha had started, back when they first got engaged and couldn't decide where to go for their honeymoon. "You can take your second wife to Cancun," she said. "Me, I want Hawaii."

The second wife was an avid rock climber, she had no menstrual cramps, she was not allergic to anything. Martha told Larry his second wife would have great big bazooms. "And a little dog." Dogs made Martha itch.

"I want a big dog," Larry said.

"Okay, your second wife will be a big dog. Don't say I didn't warn you."

Martha's second husband was an enthusiastic dishwasher. He fixed pancakes every morning. He hated watching sports and never mentioned things like wanting to skydive or dangle from a rock.

"A pansy," said Larry. "You'd give up all this for a pansy?" He flexed his muscles, wagged his eyebrows.

It was never clarified under what circumstances wife number two and husband number two would assume their positions. Martha thought of them as charms, warding off any real broken-up future. They pranced around like jesters—wife number two with her torpedo boobs, husband number two with his bug collection—like reminders of how much worse things could be. Reminders of how lucky Martha and Larry were to have each other.

And yet lately, when Martha was doing a restaurant review and was sitting all alone at some round marble table beside a fountain, she would feel suddenly, exhilaratingly available. She would write "croutons soggy, house dressing watery, waitstaff harried yet efficient" and pretend she was writing a letter to a lover, an ex or a future one—someone who was not the second husband she and Larry had invented, with his apron and his horn-rimmed glasses. She would glance around and try to catch the eye of some handsome man eating alone, like in one of those commercials for antacid. Usually there wasn't one, but the feeling—*I could have an affair*—stayed with her, singing beneath her skin.

When Larry went with her on her reviews he would mispronounce items on the menu in a thick redneck accent. "I'll have some a them cheese creeps," he'd say. "And the bull-yo-base."

And Martha would sit there giggling while the waiter or waitress smiled pathetically. No mysterious restaurant man she could have an affair with would ever say, "Gimme some a them tore-tilluhs." No mysterious restaurant man would put up with her soup cans and her ripped underwear. The thought that Larry wouldn't either made her feel a sick doom drop into her stomach like a big gray rock.

"You can take your second wife to dinner parties," she'd told him tonight. "I'm staying home."

She had spent the afternoon at a Mexican restaurant, writing him a letter that sometimes began, *There's something you need to know* and sometimes began *I don't want to scare you.* But she couldn't get much further than that. It occurred to her that she might not tell him at all; or maybe someday when they were eating breakfast she might say, "If I hadn't had that laser surgery (or freezing, or whatever they might have to do to her) ten years ago, I would be dead today. Pass the toast."

Larry begged her to come to the party. He apologized for being an insensitive lout, he told her he loved it when she ate soup out of the can, he said he was undeserving of her. He pleaded insanity. He said he would be bored stupid if she didn't come. He wanted Walter to meet her, to see how wonderful married life could be.

"Ha," said Martha, but she relented.

For the dinner party she had tried to look well put together. She'd spritzed and moussed, she'd accessorized. "Whatever you do," she warned Larry as he zipped her, "do not tell anybody what I do for a living. I don't want to be obliged to critique the fondue or whatever."

"Just say it melted in your mouth," Larry told her. "No, I won't say a word."

Martha glares at herself in Dierdre's bathroom mirror. The excessive spritzing has given her hair a grimy, lacquered look. Her green eyeliner has spread toward her temples, alien-like. She smudges off the eyeliner, then flips her head and tries to comb the goopiness out with her fingers. "Son of a bitch," she says, but she's thinking of Larry, not her hair. Is he deliberately trying to make her feel bad, as a way of getting back at her for yelling this morning? She's the one who should be getting back. Maybe instead of fighting like other couples, they'll do this—jab away at each other, leaving imperceptible bruises, until they can't get near each other without cringing.

When she goes back to the living room, everyone has changed seats. Larry is next to the maroon dress, Shelley and Walter are on the sofa with Mickey, Mickey's wife is in Martha's chair, next to Dierdre. Martha sits down beside Larry, and the maroon dress stretches around him and gives Martha a wide, insincere (it seems to Martha) smile. "There's your second wife," Martha whispers to Larry, who leans away and gives her a look that makes her wish she'd kept quiet. "Kidding," she hisses to his retreating ear.

Shelley is talking loudly. "I mean, you don't have to actually meet a person to really know them is all I'm trying to say. I knew Walter better after three months of emailing than I've known guys I *lived* with."

"How many guys'd you live with?" says Walter. "Ah ha, just kidding."

"Don't make me smack you," says Shelley, smacking him.

"Have some pie," says Dierdre, passing Martha a plate and a fork. "But if you hate it, blame *him*." She points at the Italian. "He did the pie."

Martha lifts her fork at him. She takes a bite. "It melts in my mouth," she says, smiling. The pie is too sugary. The Italian nods. He's the only one who hasn't moved. His shiny black shoes are flat on the floor and his arms are draped over the black denim angles of his knees, his left hand holding his right wrist. He seems rough yet clean, and Martha is willing to overlook his sideburns. He looks as if once he stood up, he would be appealingly lanky. Martha realizes that this is who she's been looking for in those cafés, this is the restaurant man with whom she would flirt and then have a clandestine affair. Thinking of it makes her feel guilty and nervous. He would be at the table next to hers, reading the *New York Times*, sipping espresso. He would look up at her and nod, much as he had just nodded, and it would be settled, somehow. That would be it. No mystifying, awkward small talk.

"I just want to say real quick," says Dierdre, leaning over and touching Martha briefly on the wrist, "that my sister had to get a cyst-thing lasered, and this was three years ago. And she's perfectly fine, hasn't had a problem since. She even had triplets last year."

"That sounds like a problem," says Walter.

"Well," Martha says. "I'm sure everything will be fine."

"Of course it will," says Shelley. "You want some coffee, Martha?"

"Oh! Are we out of wine?" Martha realizes that she's forgotten to get drunk. That had been her plan of action for the evening— get gleefully, blissfully drunk.

"Finish it off," Dierdre says and passes her the bottle, shaking it by the neck. "Guzzle out of the bottle if you want."

"Never mind," Martha says, feeling insulted. "Coffee would be nice, thank you."

"Is coffee okay?" says Larry. "I mean, for—"

"For someone in my condition? I think I'll live."

Larry subsides in his chair, and Martha feels a sly, familiar meanness creeping around inside her chest. She wonders how long it's been there.

"Anybody want to finish off the wine?" Dierdre is holding the bottle aloft. "Come on, don't be shy."

"Oh, give it here," says the maroon dress. She drinks it from the bottle, and Martha feels strangely jealous. *You're laid back yet uptight*, Larry had told her. *You're carefree in a cautious sort of way.* "Good stuff." The maroon dress wipes her mouth with the back of her hand. Her hair is thick, shiny black, clamped to her head like a helmet. Martha had only been partly kidding about this being Larry's second wife. If they break up, he'll end up with someone like her, perhaps he'll end up with her specifically. She's a friend of Shelley's; she would get wind of the divorce. (Or death? Martha wonders, experimentally.) She would call up and offer condolences. She would offer to be a Friend. Martha has taken note of her long fingernails. Larry likes to have his back scratched, and a pair of fingernails like that would make him very happy, she's sure.

"Why don't you-all have a dinner party?" Dierdre says to Larry.

"Yeah, we should. Shouldn't we, Martha?"

She had suggested this once and Larry had said he thought they were more of a barbecue sort of couple. Not that they'd had one of those, either.

"We should." Martha nods politely, then tries to catch the Italian's eye, to send him a mental message. She hasn't composed the message entirely yet, but then he isn't looking at her yet, either. It seems unfair that Dierdre should have a love interest like this so soon after her divorce—unless, of course, she'd had him *before* the divorce. Maybe Fred came home from work one day and there they were, Dierdre sprawled naked on the bed while the Italian rendered her tender parts in pastel.

"I found some of Fred's pot in the freezer this morning," Dierdre says. "I thought it was tea and almost made myself a cup of it."

Mickey, who hasn't spoken all night, revives suddenly and struggles up from the sofa, startling the cats off the back of it. "Hey," he says. "Hey, I can make a bong."

"You little pothead, you," says his wife.

"No, really, I can," Mickey says.

"Would you stop already?" says his wife.

"Really, you want to?" He looks around the room. "I just need a toilet paper roll."

"A gerbil chew!" squeals the maroon dress.

"And some tin foil. That's it."

"Oh," says Dierdre. "I threw it away. The pot, I mean, not the tinfoil."

"I'm sorry about him," says Mickey's wife. "What are you, in high school? He *teaches* high school, you guys. Social studies, and he's a social retard."

Mickey smiles and settles back into the sofa, his arms across his chest. His cheeks are flushed. Walter is yawning. Dierdre, the maroon dress, and Mickey's wife go into the kitchen. Shelley is mumbling, "Here, kitty kitty," waving her hand in the direction of Noggin or Pipper, Martha can't remember which. The Italian seems to be staring intently at nothing, but then Martha realizes there's a clock on the wall. The Italian wants to leave! If she were someone else, she would get up and go squat down beside him. "You want to go outside for some air?" she would say in conspiratorial tones, and he would nod, then rise to his feet, unfolding like a butterfly. They would go outside and stare at the stars and the saguaro shadows. "Sometimes," he would say, after a long, cozy silence. "Sometimes I am so *tired* of her. Of all of them." On cue, a loud cackle would pour out of the house. The Italian would wince. Then Martha would say, "Do you want to go someplace?" and they'd get into his little red car and speed off into the mountains. He would have a bottle of wine in the back seat. He would have a corkscrew.

When she had finished crying in Dr. Wang's office, Martha asked, "So assuming it's something bad, how long would it take this thing to kill me?" She had expected a vague answer: "Not for a long time," or "There's no telling," or even, "Sooner than you think." She had not expected something as specific as ten years. ("Completed progression time," Dr. Wang said. "That's just a guess.")

Martha had tried to think of herself ten years from now, lucky to be alive, and she realized that she could not picture this future or even tell what she wanted it to be. Would she be with Larry or Larry-less? Alone, or with some second husband she couldn't have predicted? It occurred to her that this future held something she hadn't thought of yet, something resistant to charms or the ghosts of future spouses. She had thought that when she told Larry, "I'll be fine. Don't worry," his concern, his love, would be the thing that trampled out all the unknown futures and sent the ghosts spinning away.

Larry is looking at her sadly. "This thing you were talking about."

"I'll be fine," says Martha, smiling beatifically, wishing she could stop feeling this way, or stop talking, or leave before everything is completely, utterly ruined.

"Why didn't you tell me?" Larry whispers.

"It's no rush," Martha says flatly. "I was going to."

And then so she won't keep doing this, saying these things, she stands up. Fast, so she can't stop to wonder what she's doing, or what they must all think of her. Larry's face flickers briefly with alarm. *Your second wife will be charming at dinner parties*, she thinks, but all she says is, "I have to get some sleep. I have to go." Larry jumps to his feet, and when he says, "We're taking off, you guys," Martha feels something between relief and despair, a strange dangling feeling that she can't identify. Dierdre finds their coats. The Italian watches them, the women wave, the men pump Larry's hand, kiss Martha's cheek. "Good luck," says everyone. "Good luck." Martha wonders what this night will become ten years from now, if she will remember that Larry's face had gone suddenly pale, or that he squeezed her shoulders on the way out the door, or that she could not stop wanting him to be afraid.

In the car driving home, Martha says, "Your second wife will be beautiful and Italian with shining helmet hair and fingernails that draw blood." When Larry doesn't say anything she tells him, "She'll throw dishes. She'll wear a cloud of hair spray. She'll drive a red Camaro. Are you paying attention?" He says he is. "You'll miss me every day of your life," she says, and she's not sure what he means when he tells her he already does.

Cool

Here's what I discover the evening after my mother leaves: if I throw a pebble into the air, bats will swoop after it. They dive toward the ground and then back up to the sky—every single time. It's like they never learn their lesson. "They think it's a bug," my father tells me when he sees what I'm doing. I didn't even know we had bats in New Hampshire. I thought bats existed only in horror movies and comic books—though I once heard my mother say, "I must have bats in my belfry," and I laughed, but my father didn't.

"Stop it, Carlene," my father calls across the lawn. The sun is almost down, and he's a shadow under the porch light. It's a hot summer evening; the air is foggy from the exterminator truck that just chugged through the neighborhood. "Don't be mean to them. They're going to get you."

I throw another pebble; there's a silent swooping of wings. Sometimes one bat comes, sometimes two.

"I'm serious," my father says. "They'll get you."

"I find that highly doubtful," I say and throw another pebble. When I was little, I used to think every rock in the yard was an arrowhead, but now I know better. All the interesting artifacts are long gone, dug up and stuck in museums no one visits except on field trips. I throw a bigger rock, and two bats swoop this time, in figure eights. It's deep dusk now, the sky is almost purple, and I can hear the whish of cars headed toward the turnpike. As long as the bats aren't getting tired of this game, neither am I. "I'm going to be here for a while," I tell my father, so he disappears into the house. I wonder if he's packed up my mother's clothes for her like he said he would. I wonder how many of my clothes have ended up in her closet over the past couple of years, and then I decide I don't care. She can have all my Old Navy miniskirts if she wants them. Good riddance.

On my fifteenth birthday last month, my father gave me a key chain with mace, and a card saying I was now subscribed to *National Geographic*. He left both outside my door in the middle of the night, and when I thanked him in the morning he nodded and saluted with a piece of toast as he went out the front door to his job at the water department.

My mother gave me the black boots I'd asked for, but with a higher heel than I wanted. I knew that was because she wanted to wear them, too. I thought it was great that my mother and I wore the same size, and that she dyed her hair as blond as mine, and that she took me to R-rated movies. Sometimes we'd pass a flask of root beer schnapps back and forth while we ate popcorn.

"You're lucky you have such a cool mom," my friend Sarah said once. "I know it," I told her. "She's, like, my best friend." And that made Sarah pout because she thought *she* was my best friend.

On my birthday morning, my mother and I tried on my boots and took turns doing spins in them. "Do I *have* to take tennis lessons?" I asked, because I knew she would say no. Tennis lessons were my father's idea. It was the first week of summer vacation, and I was supposed to be keeping busy: not just tennis lessons at the Y, but also babysitting the mutant children next door, studying for the PSATs, and reading great literature—none of which appealed to me. My mother told me I could come help her at the Zumba studio, but I told her, "I'm not feeling it," and she said that was fine. "Chill out for a while," she said. "Oh, and this isn't your only present, by the way. Have a seat, stop twirling for a sec."

"Yeah?" I had my hopes up for an iPad, even though my father had told me to wait until Christmas. "What is it?"

She reached into the pocket of her sundress and pulled out an envelope, which she slid across the kitchen table to me like it was an offer I couldn't refuse. Inside were three tickets for the following week: Slippery Rick at the Hampton Beach Casino Ballroom. "*Well?*" she said, her eyes bright.

"Well," I said. Slippery Rick was a Boston band that was big in the eighties: five guys in leather pants with a lot of chest hair. They had that one hit song you still hear at weddings, the one that makes the older crowd get up and dance like idiots. I actually like that song, but mostly I knew that my mother was in love with Slippery Rick—she still had a signed poster, rolled up in a plastic tube in the hall closet—so I hugged her and said, "This is *very* cool. Thank you."

"I know, right?" she said. "I haven't seen them since, like, 1990!"

I stared at the three tickets. "Dad's going, too?" My father, as far as I knew, was more of a Pixies fan. That was the poster he had in his dorm room, and my mom would rip it down or draw mustaches on it. My parents met in college when my mother fell asleep on my father at a party. "True love is mysterious," he told me once, with a big grin. But that was a long time ago, and he doesn't grin like that anymore, about anything.

"No, of course your father isn't going," my mother snapped. At some point, she had stopped calling him by his actual name— which is Rick, funnily enough. "I thought you could ask that boy you like." She held up a hand. "I don't mean *like*-like. I mean that lab partner boy who likes music."

"Jason," I said. I could feel my face getting hot, so I took a swig of orange juice. Jason let me do all the worm dissecting because I found it fascinating, but I hated cutting up the frogs so he did all that. He wore big, old-fashioned headphones. Sarah called him "nerdy-cool." Once, he put his headphones on my ears, and I didn't even know what the hell I was listening to, but I bobbed my head and smiled and said it was great. He'd given me his phone number, saying, "In case you run across some frogs that need dissecting," but I hadn't ever called or texted him. "I guess Jason might want to go," I told my mother.

At nine thirty, I decide it's time to leave the bats alone. If it were up to them, they would keep chasing rocks all night. *Why don't you figure it out, bats?* I ask them in my head, but they don't answer.

I can feel them waiting for another fake bug to fly up in the air, and it suddenly seems cruel for me to keep getting their hopes up.

The house is silent: just the hum of the fridge, the rumble of the ice maker. The dishes are done. Nothing really seems different except my mother isn't sitting in the living room, wrapped up in a blue blanket, watching HBO Go. She started sleeping on the sofa a couple of months ago.

One morning in May she peeked her head above the cushions as I was heading out the door to school and said, "Is your father still here?"

"No, he left already."

"Good. You want to go shopping with me, and I'll write you a note saying you're sick?"

So of course I threw my book bag down and said, "Why oh hell yes."

It's hard to believe my parents got along before they were my parents, but I've seen photographic evidence: my father standing with his arm around my mother and smoking something that does not look like a cigarette. He had one of those haircuts that's business in the front and party in the back. Now he has balding in the front and business in the back. Once, during an argument about who knows what, my mother yelled, "Maybe I should have passed out on your roommate Steve." And my father said, very calmly, "I wish you had, Jenny." He went upstairs and slammed the door, and that's when she started sleeping on the sofa.

My bedroom is upstairs and down the hall from the master bedroom. I used to have my own bathroom until my mother started using it, filling the counters with her Clinique moisturizers and mascaras and Pink Beaches lipstick. It's all still there—I guess you don't have to look good in rehab—so I push it off the counter and into the trash with a clatter. For a moment, I wonder if the noise woke my father, but then I hear low, even snores from behind his closed door.

I put on my sweats and get into bed, but the house feels too hot so I get up to crack the room's only window, which has a screen that's half-rotted out of its frame and waves like a sheet when the air moves. Outside: an oak tree, the distant neighbors' houses glinting through the trees. A moon glowing like a big toenail. When I get back in bed, the curtains move in the breeze and I think of ghosts. My grandparents are dead, my father's brother died last year, my mother's only sister died when I was ten. It's comforting, thinking of all those dead people who are probably gazing down at me with kind smiles, shaking their heads because everything is so screwed up.

At first I think the ghosts have heard me thinking and are giving me a sign—a flutter of pale curtain—but then I realize the fluttering is more like thrashing, and it's not a ghostly hand doing it but a bat, which is suddenly in my room—so much bigger and clumsier than it seemed outside, a winged rat flapping in crazed circles. I'm out of bed and down the hall, shouting, "Crap crap crap," and sounding so much like my mother that even before he opens his door, my father is calling, "Jenny? Jenny?" and his voice is desperate and hopeful.

"No," I gasp when he comes staggering into the glare of the hallway. "You were right—it came to get me."

I felt like an idiot texting Jason—*I've got tix to Slippery Rick! U in?*—but he was very excited and called me right back. He had two of their albums on cassette, and he told me they were "an icon of the big-hair era," and then he went on about how they influenced some other bands I'd never heard of. His mother called my mother and they talked for ages on the kitchen phone. "I assured her there would be no gun play or cocaine and that I'd have him home before midnight," my mother said and winked. Arrangements were made. And on a balmy June evening, we picked him up at his house on Haines Street. He was waiting on the curb. His mother waved from the front window, and we all waved back.

I moved from the front seat to the back, and my mother drove like a chauffeur. She was wearing her hair up in a fluffy ponytail, like mine, and she'd borrowed one of my miniskirts and a halter top and my birthday boots. Before we'd left the house, we'd admired ourselves in my bathroom mirror, and she'd said, "We are a couple of girls with some great tits," and I agreed we were. When we'd headed out the door, my father had turned down the TV long enough to call, "Have fun!" and my mother had called back, "You bet we will!"

In his khaki shorts with his hair sticking up in a fake Mohawk, Jason looked different than he did in school. He had a little silver hoop earring. When he saw me staring, he grinned and said, "Didn't know I was in a boy band, did you?" He laughed, I laughed, my mother laughed. I felt like I'd had about five Diet Cokes, filled up with carbonation and caffeine.

My mother was chatty and charming, which made me chatty and charming, too. She and Jason compared favorite bands and I pretended not to know who any of them were. "Isn't it a good thing we're exposing her to some culture?" my mother asked, twinkling into the rearview mirror.

Jason's arm brushed mine as he said, "Oh, definitely. I just hope it's not too late."

It's exactly fifty-nine minutes to Hampton Beach on 93, but the drive seemed to take exactly four minutes. At one point, Jason leaned over and whispered in my ear, "You have such a cool mom."

I nodded.

He leaned back and whispered, "You're cool, too." I was already having the best time of my entire life, and I didn't care if we kept driving forever and never went to see Slippery Rick. Which, it turns out, would have been a much better option than what actually happened.

My father is digging through the hall closet, tossing stuff onto the floor: ski poles, a boogie board, my mother's parka, a dust pan. "Here," he calls from the depths of the closet, tossing out my tennis racket and the long plastic tube holding my mom's signed Slippery Rick poster. He's wearing a blue ski mask, and I'm so startled I start to laugh. He doesn't say anything, just picks up the poster tube and dust pan. "You should stay out here," he says, and his eyes are hard like a burglar's.

"No," I tell him. I'm already putting on my own ski mask. It's occurred to me how serious and dangerous this mission is. Everybody knows about rabid bats, about the horror of rabies shots. A girl in Hudson got bit a few years ago and almost died, or that was the rumor anyway. I pick up my tennis racket, the one my father bought me months ago and which I haven't used once. It feels good in my hands, and I decide that if I survive this rabid bat attack, I will actually start taking lessons.

"I'll go in first, and you shut the door behind us," my father says. His mouth looks redder than usual, the way it does when he's skiing. I wonder if I look different, too, behind my pink mask. It feels too tight, as if my head has grown since the last time we went skiing—but that was almost five years ago, so of course my head is bigger. *I have an adult-sized head* is what I'm thinking, even as I follow my father into my bedroom and slam the door. *I have an adult-sized head* is the weird thing I'm thinking as I duck to avoid the bat flailing up toward the ceiling light. It swoops around the center of the room and then up toward the ceiling again, its wings fluttering in a way that seems both pretty and creepy. My father is spinning in circles, too, making noises like *Ahhh* and *Uhhh* as he swings the poster tube like a baseball bat.

"Get out, you stupid bat!" I yell, whirling with my racket. The bat won't listen. I imagine what it would be like to always have a bat in my room, that I'd have to get used to it flying above me while I sleep, and get used to bat poop falling on my head, and then I'd have to feed it, like a pet, so that it didn't die in midair. Maybe it would calm down eventually and just hang on my wall, its little wings curled up around it. When my mother came home from rehab, I'd take her into my room and say, "This is what happens when you leave: we adopt a bat." And she'd want me to get rid of it, but by then I'd love the bat and wouldn't want it to leave. I'd tie a little string to it and take it to school, and everyone would think I was a freak because I had a pet bat instead of having a crazy mother.

"You know it's not her fault," my father said to me before she left for rehab. He'd come into my room and was sitting on the edge of my bed while I stood and stared at him.

"I know," I said, even though I didn't know. But now I think, yes, it is. It's her fault that I was so bored and lonely I taunted a bat into my room. It's her fault my father and I are wearing ski masks in summer because we're scared and don't know what we're supposed to do.

My father swings again; my desk lamp teeters. Then I hear the thud of the poster tube hitting the bat, and the thing falls to the carpet. I haven't even caught my breath before my father scoops it up with the dust pan and throws it out the window, and I don't know what I'm doing when I pull off my ski mask and fly out of my room and down the stairs and out the back door, my father calling after me as I run.

Our seats were so close to the stage that I could see the sweat on Slippery Rick's face, and I could feel the drums in my chest. "It's all the original band!" my mother screamed into one ear, while Jason screamed, "They rock!" into the other. I admit that when they first came onstage, in a swarm of strobe lights, my heart sank a little: five middle-aged bald men with beer bellies, wearing leather pants that didn't have quite enough stretch. The lead singer, Slippery Rick himself, was wearing glasses. His once-flowing hair was now tied back in a scrawny gray ponytail. But then the drums started, and the guitars, and the screaming all around us. People my mother's age were leaping up and down like maniacs, so we leapt up and down like maniacs, too.

My only concert before this one was an *American Idol* tour at the Manchester Arena three years ago, with my friends Sarah and Megan, my mom and Megan's mom. Megan's mom was still wearing her lawyer clothes and she didn't get up to dance once, just sat frowning at her iPhone. When my mother offered her a swig from her root beer schnapps flask, Megan's mom said, "Are you insane?" According to my mother, Megan's mom had "a stick up her ass." She was perfectly nice, but she definitely wasn't a cool mom. Not too long after that, my mom took me and Megan to the mall, and in the food court she bought us both soft pretzels and told Megan that someday, if she ever needed to get an abortion but couldn't tell her own mother, "I'll drive you to the clinic and never tell a soul." She raised a hand and made a zipper-motion on her lips. Megan told her mother, who had the most uncool of reactions, and after that Megan and I didn't hang out anymore.

Jason was holding his iPhone above his head and yelling "Woohoo!" over and over. I thought of getting out my own phone and then I thought no, now I can ask him to email me the video, and I felt proud of myself and started screaming along to the lyrics, even though I couldn't make out what they were. It didn't matter, I realized, because Slippery Rick was the best band in the entire world. I understood all of it—the love songs *and* the shouting songs. It was all for me, and about me, and when Jason grabbed my hand during one of the ballads I literally thought I might pass out. As in, everything went gray and swimmy. I knew I was about to be kissed—not quite yet, but very, very soon. And not kissed like Greg Howard had kissed me at the roller rink when I was twelve—all slobber and braces—but movie-kissed, with tongues and hair-stroking and moaning. *I would do anything for you*, I thought—and I meant it 100 percent, even though Jason had already let go of my hand, and even though that was what Slippery Rick was singing right at that moment.

At what point did I realize my mother was gone? It might have been just before the second encore, or it might have been when the lights went up and everyone looked around blinking and smiling at the now-empty stage. But I didn't care. I knew where the car was, and I knew she wouldn't leave without us. In fact, as Jason and I joined the crowd moving toward the exit, past the Slippery Rick T-shirt displays and then out onto Ocean Boulevard, I thought she was being an especially cool mom, letting us be alone for a while.

"My ears are ringing!" I said, when we were standing on the pavement in front of the casino.

"What?" he said, and we both laughed. The night air was full of neon and the smells of Italian sausage, fried dough, and the sea. We let ourselves be swept down the boulevard, past McDonald's and the sub shop and the Candy Corner, and I swung my hand close to his, waiting for him to take it. *Kiss me, kiss me*, I thought. Across the boulevard, the sea was crashing and couples were strolling on the beach—all of them holding hands, from what I could see.

"They were great," Jason said. We had stopped walking and were standing in front of Playland, the sounds of video games pouring out all around us. A bearded man was trying to fish a teddy bear out of a big yellow machine with a hook while a girl in a pink bikini watched.

"They were *so* great," I said. I was about to work up my nerve to ask if he wanted to go across the street to the beach when I saw myself just ahead on the sidewalk, leaning against a trashcan, kissing a guy in a Slippery Rick tour jacket. My hands were in his hair and his were in mine, and I teetered a little in my new birthday boots, and my halter top looked like it was starting to come undone. I was moaning and the man was moaning, and when the real me let out a cry, my mother turned and blinked. I could smell the liquor on her breath from two feet away. The guy—goateed, crooked teeth—grinned and said, "Hey." He blew cigarette smoke into the air.

"Oh my God," Jason said, and nobody else spoke for what felt like a long time. We walked in silence to the car. My mother wobbled and grabbed my wrist. I pulled away.

"I'm so—" she said, and then she didn't seem to know what to say next.

"Give me your keys," Jason said to her. He sounded kind but stern. I didn't bother pointing out that he was too young to have a driver's license, and neither did my mother. She handed the keys over without a word.

Jason and I sat in the front seat, my mother sat sniffling in the back. The drive that had seemed to take four minutes now seemed like four hours. When he took the exit toward Nashua, my mother said, "I've sobered up. Go on to your house and I'll take it from there." She sounded hoarse, but she did sound sober. He pulled into his driveway and hopped out without saying good-bye, leaving the door open and the engine running.

"I'm sorry!" my mother called, as he disappeared inside his house. She got into the front seat beside me. "Your father and I once had a great passion," she said, so I got out and slammed into the back seat to let her know she was just a chauffeur. I didn't mind when she talked about my tits, or even when she told Megan she'd take her to get an abortion, but hearing her talk about passion with my father—after she'd just been making out with a damn roadie—was too much.

That night, I heard her crying, my father shouting. The next morning, when I came downstairs, they were both drinking coffee at the kitchen table. She looked younger than when she dressed like me—wearing a pink cardigan and khaki pants, her hair smooth on her shoulders. My father looked younger, too, weirdly enough, with his clothes all rumpled and his hair sticking up. I could almost, *almost* see the two people from old photographs who used to love each other.

"Your mother is going into a program," my father said, and she nodded. "We won't be able to talk to her for a week, and we won't be able to visit for two weeks."

"How long will she be gone?" I couldn't even look at her.

"A month, maybe two," said my father. He took a sip of coffee. "Maybe three."

At first I don't see it, but then I do: lying on the grass in the puddle of light coming through my bedroom window. My father is calling down to me: "Don't touch it, Carlene. It's probably just stunned."

I'm not an idiot. Of course I'm not going to touch it. It seems so much smaller than the pterodactyl that was swooping around my room, just a teeny mouse with little fairy wings. I realize I'm standing over it with the tennis racket raised. I won't even squash spiders, but I want to kill this creature for scaring me. My heart is racing as fast as it did when Jason held my hand, and I think of my mother kissing that roadie with her eyes closed. I'll bet she was imagining he was Slippery Rick, or maybe that he was my father when they were young, and I wonder if my mother went to rehab for drinking or for passion, because apparently there's no difference between love and craziness. Maybe that's what I've learned from all of this.

But that's a lie. I haven't learned anything, any more than the bats learn not to chase rocks in the air. My father is calling my name. Below my raised racket, the little bat's eyes open, and they're round and black and shiny as oil. We stare at each other, our tiny, stunned hearts pounding, and I wonder which of us is more terrified of what's coming next.

HILDA

Sometimes when Hilda finds herself awake in the predawn dark, she thinks about the funeral parlor/hardware store she and Oliver had run back in Glendive, Montana, all those years ago. She can smell the polished wooden coffins, hear the distant hum of Oliver's power saw. She sees her younger self leaning over a body to apply foundation, powder, and rouge, brushing and styling the hair. Sometimes she can see the faces but usually not. There had been that one terrible woman who had eaten ant poison, her lips blackened and blistered. That was the only time Hilda had ever felt afraid, and she'd run next door to find Oliver standing on the top rung of a ladder and reaching for a paint can. She had held the ladder for him and then gone back to the dead woman.

The woman's husband came to the funeral parlor and peered into the casket and said, "She looks nice." He was a small man in a tan suit; Hilda can see him clearly behind her eyelids as she lies in her bed in Orlando under the whir-whir of the ceiling fan. His face is furrowed in sorrow, but his eyes are large and blank, like a child's. She can't remember where the funeral was held, or the woman's name, and sometimes all she can see are those black lips, the way the lipstick slid right off them, the way they seemed about to open, and apologize.

Gust calls her up to say, "I have an umbrella lamp you're gonna love. Seventeen dollars." Gust is eighty-five, eleven years her senior. A month ago she bought a desk from him, and he got her phone number from her check.

"I don't think I need a lamp," she starts to say, but Gust interrupts.

"You haven't seen it. You can't know if you don't see it."

In the past month, Gust has called her seven times to inform her of things she would love: an ottoman, a crate of *Life* magazines dating from 1955, a print of Monet's water lilies, a set of five Time Life books, a blender (which doesn't work), a green flower vase, and a transistor radio. Each time Hilda drove her truck (Oliver's old truck) to Winter Park. When the items were heavy, Gust banged on his neighbor's door until a weary undershirt-wearing man in his thirties emerged and hauled the desk (or ottoman or crate of magazines) to Hilda's truck. When Hilda got home, she rapped on her neighbor Anna Dietz's door to ask to borrow her grandson. The first time Anna Dietz had been amused, but lately she's been saying things like, "Don't you have enough junk in your house already, Hilda? Do you want to be one of those hoarders?"

"I don't want to turn into one of those hoarders," Hilda says now, and Gust says, "I made something for you." She can picture him in his small, cluttered house standing in the kitchen and waggling his eyebrows at the wall. He does that whenever Hilda seems reluctant or says she has to be going, as if his eyebrows are transmitting hypnotic signals just for her. She can't tell if she feels sorry for him or actually wants to see him. Or maybe she really *would* like this lamp; there's a dim corner of her bedroom that could use some light.

"Give me an hour," she says.

Every Sunday, Hilda takes a walk around the pond in her backyard and clears away the water hyacinths around the boat, tosses some saltines to the ducks, and then goes inside and opens a can of tuna, slices a tomato, and reads the Sunday paper.

In August, a month before driving to Gust's apartment for the umbrella lamp, she had felt a deep, abiding boredom—with the pond, the house, the weather, Anna Dietz. ("You just go on to church without me, Anna," she said and was both annoyed and pleased that Anna didn't offer to come over after and see how she was feeling.) The air was clammy and the sky hung like boiled sheets behind her banana tree. She put on some water and skimmed through the paper to see if anyone had blown up Hartford, Connecticut, where her daughter lives; or Washington, D.C., where her son lives; or if any planes had crashed anywhere. Hilda has never been on a plane and needs a ready supply of reasons when her children try to cajole her into flying instead of taking Amtrak.

She flipped then to obituaries, a habit from when she and Oliver had run Anderson's Funeral Parlor & Hardware. It had been her job to make the dead look presentable, and many people had praised her talents and inquired as to whether she would also provide such services to the living. Hilda always declined.

After obituaries (no one she knew), she turned to classifieds because it occurred to her that what she really wanted was a desk. If she had a desk, she would be more inclined to write letters to her sisters in North Dakota, her grandchildren, her children. If she had a desk, she would sort through her photos and make labels for them and file them in a drawer. Perhaps she would write her memoirs: nothing fancy, just tidbits about her life, like the time she saw a meteorite land in her backyard when she was nine, or how she and Oliver drove five hours to the hospital in North Dakota when little Linda got a curtain hook stuck in her throat.

Hilda ran her finger down the page to home furnishings. She wasn't sure what a futon was, but she suspected it was nothing that she wanted. There were televisions and VCRs, sleeper sofas and queen-size water beds. Then her eyes fell on "Moving Sale: lamps, sofa, television, desk, bookcase. MUCH MUCH MORE!!! Sunday 9am to 2pm." There was a Winter Park address. And so Hilda drove to Winter Park.

Gust's front door is propped open with a ceramic terrier.

"Hello?" says Hilda, leaning in from the porch. "Gust?" She isn't one for shouting into other people's houses. She raps on the screen door, then pushes the doorbell. It makes a sound like one of the frogs in her pond. The house is dark and smells like cabbage. From somewhere within it a toilet flushes.

"I suppose I've come for the umbrella lamp," she calls. "Why, hello there."

Out of the dimness Gust is coming toward her in his stiff, forward-tilted gait, like someone who has thrown away his cane and is trying to prove he no longer needs it. He pulls the screen door open and says, "I knew you'd come. Did you bring your checkbook?"

"I'll look at the lamp and then decide if I need my checkbook." She's decided it's time to put an end to this. Yesterday, she'd asked Anna Dietz if her grandson might need any old *Life* magazines for a school project, and she'd laughed and said, "He'll be over this afternoon." Ronny Dietz is a tall and scrawny boy with crabapple muscles and a tiny mustache, and he cheerfully hauled away the crate of magazines. Later that afternoon, she saw them sitting by the dumpster on the curb.

Gust is wearing a pair of bright yellow Bermuda shorts and a green T-shirt with palm trees on it, a variation on the same thing he wears whenever she comes over. Today, she notices with alarm, the shorts have a golf ball–sized hole in the rear. She can see Gust's pale skin winking behind the fabric as she follows him into the living room, and she has the distinct impression he's laughing at her, though silently.

The living room is, as always, teetering with boxes and books, lamps and knickknacks. A stationary bicycle that seems to be from the 1970s is draped with vests and suit coats. A lime-green sofa is stacked with rusty-looking pots and pans. When she'd come over the first time, answering his ad, he'd explained, "My son in Apopka wants me to move into the room above his garage. I've brought everything out here, you see. To make it easier to sell and to pack."

"What a wonderful idea," she'd said, wondering who would want to buy such junk. The desk, however, had seemed solid enough, so she hauled it home where it still sits wrapped in twine in her living room. Then Gust had produced a small wooden peg game from seemingly nowhere and said, "I make these. I'll bet you can't get down to one peg." That was how she'd ended up staying for an entire hour, and she still didn't manage to get down to one peg.

"First of all, I have a present for you," Gust says now. She knows what it is, of course, and still tries to show surprise when he places the triangle of wood in her hand. "One game," he says.

"Thank you very much, but I have someone waiting on me at home. I'll take it with me and play it there." She holds the triangle steady so as not to tumble out the red pegs, and that's when Gust points and says, "Here's your lamp. Take out your checkbook."

It's not an umbrella at all. And this lamp hadn't been here earlier, she's certain of it. She's certain she would have noticed the bright red flounce of what is clearly a skirt, and the porcelain fishnet thighs emerging from it, ending in red high heels. The legs are crossed so that the torso-less, headless female is standing in a position that looks vaguely balletic, but mostly obscene.

"I don't think you *are* moving," Hilda says. "I don't know if you even have a son. I think you're lonely and you like to fool with people."

Gust ignores her. He's leaning down and plugging the lamp in. When the skirt lights up he says, "Do you like it?"

Hilda says, "I do not," and marches out the door into the damp September afternoon, slams into her truck, and tosses the peg game on the seat beside her, sending the red pegs rolling every which way.

"Did that old man trick you into buying any more of his crap?" her son asks on the phone from Washington, D.C. He calls her every

Sunday afternoon at three o'clock. Her daughter lives in Hartford and calls less frequently and at odd times, late at night or too early in the morning, whenever she can "grab a spare minute," as she says, from the twins. Hilda hasn't mentioned Gust to her daughter, only because Linda talks too much and too fast, and Hilda can't get a word in edgewise. But Brian, her son, is prone to long silences that need to be filled, so she made the mistake of telling him not only about the desk, but about the magazines, the radio, etcetera.

"He never tricked me," she says. "It's a perfectly good desk."

"Maybe he has ulterior motives," says Brian, and Hilda closes her eyes and tries not to think of those porcelain thighs, those arched feet under the red ceramic skirt.

"Well, I'm not going over there anymore," she tells him. "I have enough junk, as Anna Dietz keeps telling me."

Maybe it's a sign, an omen, a message? Or maybe it's simply what happens when you get old, images from the past leaking into your consciousness like rain through a crack in the roof. Surely there are other, more pleasant memories she can conjure: young Oliver when he showed up at her boarding house with his boxes of leather shoes; their daughter in her confirmation dress; Hilda's fiftieth birthday party in Key West, dancing to Elvis songs under the moon. But she keeps finding herself back at the funeral parlor, twenty-eight years old and applying makeup to the ant poison woman. Hilda has no idea how old that woman was—although certainly she must have known at some point. She must have known the woman's name, at least.

It wasn't unusual for her to be at the funeral parlor late. Sometimes the embalmer (his name completely lost to memory) didn't finish until after seven o'clock, and Hilda would finish washing the dinner dishes and either drive or, depending on the weather, walk the four blocks from their house to downtown. On this night she had walked and Oliver had come, too, the two of them wearing matching red scarves (the image arrives fully formed, another drop of rain through the roof) that she'd knitted the previous Christmas. It must have been autumn. A sharp wind was blowing in from the Badlands. They'd waved and gone into the separate entrances.

"I never asked about his wife," Hilda says to Anna Dietz over fried shrimp at Morrison's Cafeteria. "I should have inquired, don't you think? I suppose I thought it would be nosy."

"He would have talked your ear off," Anna says. "Just making up stories for attention. He's clearly senile." She forks a crusty shrimp into a mound of tartar sauce.

Hilda supposes this is possible, but she hadn't intended for her description of Gust to lead to the assumption of senility. A sick and juvenile sense of humor, definitely loneliness. "Perhaps his wife left him," Hilda muses, stirring the melting ice cubes around in her iced tea. "And now he just likes inviting women over and fooling with them."

"A dirty old crazy man!" Anna says. She swallows a mouthful of shrimp and announces, "I wouldn't go back there if I was you." Then she launches into a long complaint about Ronny's mother, how she's dating another terrible man, a truck driver this time, not that Anna minds having Ronny around, since he's such a delightful boy. She doesn't ask Hilda about her own children or grandchildren, because lunch with Anna is always about Anna. Hilda has known her for almost thirty years; she and Oliver and Anna and Thomas used to play bridge occasionally, and afterward Oliver would complain that Thomas cheated. Oliver was a sore loser, though, so Hilda was never sure if she believed him.

They had been arguing. "Fine," Hilda said, slamming the dishes in the sink—not washing them after all—grabbing her sheepskin jacket and red scarf. The air smelled of distant bonfires. A sharp wind stung her cheeks. Oliver had hurried after her: "We're not finished!" They'd walked briskly down the dark streets, turned downtown to the rows of stores. Their building was on the corner; the hardware store was the street entrance; the funeral parlor was around the back.

"We are," she said, and they went into their separate entrances.

Later, as she held the ladder for him, he said, "Are you finished being mad now?" and she wasn't but she said yes and then went back to the dead woman.

What on earth could she have been so angry about? Linda was four years away, Brian two years after that. In five years they would sell the business to another funeral-home owner, who would turn the hardware store into a furniture store. They would move to Florida for the warm air; she would stay at home with the children; Oliver would buy Green's Building Supplies and work fourteen-hour days for over twenty years until, at sixty-five, he would simply not wake up one Sunday morning. Hilda was up for three hours before she thought to nudge him and see if he wanted any tea. His skin was cool, cheeks pale, brows slightly furrowed as if he was puzzled about something. The coroner estimated that he'd been dead for three hours, but then said it could have been four.

Her children have little curiosity about their Montana life. Linda doesn't care to hear the story about how she swallowed a drapery hook one February afternoon, and they had to drive through a blizzard to get her to a hospital in North Dakota. When Oliver asked if they wanted to go see Little Bighorn, thirteen-year-old Brian had said it was a shameful part of American history and that Native Americans should never have been slaughtered. "Not to mention the buffalo," he added.

Many years ago, when Linda was visiting and they were driving to Disney World with the twins, Linda said wistfully, "I suppose I'd like to see the mountains where I was born someday," and Hilda had nearly driven off the road.

"Have you never listened to a word your father and I said, ever?" she demanded. The twins had started to cry. "There are no mountains there. It's flat, hard desert. It's like the moon. The Badlands are just outside of town. No fuzzy *Sound of Music* mountains, do you hear me?"

"Geez," said Linda.

Hilda had no idea why this had upset her so, except that it seemed to confirm everything she'd feared about her children: they'd never cared at all about their past—about her past, really—and the few times they'd asked her questions ("Did you ever find fossils in Montana?"), they'd done so for their own devices ("Can I have one for my science report?"). She had been thinking that if she wrote her memoirs, they would at least read them someday—

after her death, perhaps—but she is starting to understand that this is not necessarily the case.

On a Thursday night, the phone rings and wakes Hilda from a dream that seems to gallop away into a fog. It's Linda, talking already before Hilda manages to say hello. "Finally a minute to catch my breath," she is saying. "Jill is at band practice, and Rosy has ballet, so Jim and I are finally alone, but I wanted to call and say hi."

Hilda manages to sit up and look at the clock glowing by her bedside. It's 8:45 p.m. "Slow early," she says, the slippery words striking her as wrong and not-wrong at the same time. "I thought it was midnight."

"You obviously need more excitement in your life!" Linda says. "So hop on a plane and come visit."

Hilda flicks on the bedside light. "I'm not going to hop on a plane. I'll take a train if you like." Although just the thought of that thirty-hour Amtrak trip, all those towns sliding by the window, makes her achy and exhausted.

"Or," Linda says, her voice a pitch too high, "you could pack up and move north! You like the north." She says this as if "the north" is a flavor of ice cream. It occurs to Hilda that Brian has been telling her about Gust, making her out to be a crazy, hoarding old coot. "We don't have any bears for you to shoot, though. I was telling Jim the other day about your bear."

Hilda rubs her forehead. She has absolutely no idea what Linda is taking about, "your bear." In the long silence that follows (Linda drops the phone and shouts from a distance, "I'm here! Trying to wash dishes and talk!"), a memory begins to reform itself enough for Hilda to know for certain that she never shot a bear, though she lied and said she did.

"I will keep that in mind," Hilda says, coolly, when Linda is back. "Thank you for your call. I'm sure you need to get back to Jim now."

"You bet," says Linda. "Nighty night."

She had shot *at* a bear, in the general direction of a bear, the one time she and Oliver had gone deer hunting together. They'd seen a rustling in the trees, a flash of brown, and Oliver said, "Wouldn't you like a bearskin rug?" She raised the rifle and shot, the sound of the blast shocking them both. They watched the bear lumber off, and Oliver said, "I think you got it," though they both knew she didn't. She hadn't actually cared for deer hunting (Oliver had killed a small buck), the mess and the violence of it, or for the glass-eyed head that stared down from their living room wall for years afterward.

Perhaps she had bragged to the children one day to prove she was brave, that she'd been someone before she was their mother. She'd wanted them to respect her so they would do their chores: "I killed a bear, so don't you dare track mud through the house!" Was that the sort of thing she would say? She has no idea.

The next day she walks over to Anna Dietz's house and asks if Ronny would like a small desk. Anna's house looks as if it was decorated by a five-year-old, stuffed with velvet pillows, dolls, and shiny figurines. It gives Hilda a headache just being inside; she always feels as if she's about to topple into something breakable.

"I don't know that he'd want a desk," Anna says. "But he'll take it to the curb for you."

"It's too nice for the curb," Hilda says. "Oh, never mind. He can do what he wants." The house feels oppressive; the ceiling fan is chugging hot air around in circles. "Come for a walk with me."

Outside, Anna seems even more tan than she does indoors. Her shoulders are the deep reddish brown that comes from having been sunburned her entire life. The pond is stagnant and the ducks are hiding in the long grass; the air is full of whirring insects dodging at their heads in a way that makes Hilda feel under attack. "Remember when that lake went all the way past the grove of trees?" she says.

"It's not a lake," Anna says, waving her fingers at the swarms of insects as if saying hello. "It's a swamp. It hasn't been a lake for years."

Hilda swats at a mosquito that's alighted on her cheek. The wrinkled skin there is solid, firm, as if trying to protect the body's increasingly fragile contents. The embalmer they'd hired back in Montana once bragged of his work: "When I'm done with them, you could ship them to China."

Hilda has long since given up on powdering her own face—it just settles into the wrinkles—and contents herself with a swipe of rose-colored lipstick and a dab of blush. Those things, she had told Oliver, went a long way toward making a person seem healthy, no matter how dead they were. He'd laughed at that.

"It's Ronny," Anna says, when they're standing at the crabgrass between their yards. The sky is gathering into rain clouds, and a spit of moisture strikes Hilda just below her eye. "You said Ricky. You asked if Ricky wanted your desk."

"Dear God, I did not," says Hilda. "I know Ronny's name."

"I know you do," Anna says. "Just the other day, I lost my keys for an entire hour." She gives Hilda's upper arm a quick bear-claw squeeze that Hilda supposes is meant to be reassuring.

When she gets back inside, her answering machine says she has seven missed calls, no messages. The phone rings again, and she watches the red number flash to eight. When the phone rings yet again, she answers it, and Gust says, "I've moved, and I'd like you to come over to see me. We can bake cookies."

"What?" she says.

"Cookies," he shouts. "Get a pencil and write this down." She doesn't get a pencil.

"It's going to rain," she says. "I don't like to drive in the rain." Outside, the wind is thrashing her banana tree.

"Not now. Tomorrow."

Perhaps he's lost his mind, she thinks. Perhaps she should call Social Services, Human Services, whoever it is that deals with crazy old people. Does he even have a son?

"Here's the address." He rattles off a street in Apopka. "Two o'clock." He waits for her to say okay, and then he hangs up.

The husband had stared down at his wife in her yellow satin-lined coffin. Her hair was dark and curled, the two sides meeting in a point at her chin. She was wearing a lacy white dress.

"You did a good job on her," the husband said. "She looks nice."

"Oh," said Hilda, and she brought a hand to her throat. She thought of the embalmer's words: You could ship her to China. "I wish I *could* ship her to China," she'd said to Oliver, and shuddered. There was only so much she could do, really; the face was ruined. The lips were black under the lipstick. "I'm so sorry, but I did my best," she said to the husband, and immediately she understood that was the wrong thing to say.

She had shaken the man out of whatever daze he had been in. He'd probably been seeing his wife's real face instead of this one. Now his eyes seemed to focus, and he blanched. Hilda knew what she had done. She should have said, "Thank you." She should have said, "She looks beautiful," the lie he was already telling himself.

That night, while she sobbed on the sofa, Oliver cooked a supper she couldn't eat, and he washed the dishes and put them away. He tucked her into bed and smoothed back her hair and said, "You didn't mean anything by it." That night she told him she thought she wasn't cut out for this line of work, that maybe she should put makeup on living people who could look in the mirror and tell her exactly what they thought about what'd she'd done to them.

But she didn't. The next day she was back powdering the face of an old lady from church, and then who knew how many dead faces after that. The relatives always told her their loved ones looked like they were sleeping, and Hilda always agreed that they did.

The steps are steep and made of slippery metal, and she finds herself wondering why on earth an eighty-five-year-old man would live in a garage apartment. Then again, it seems Gust was at least telling the truth, that he isn't (at least entirely) senile. In the house below, someone is watching television; Hilda can make out a hairy, tanned leg resting on an ottoman. She has dressed in her pink-and-white pantsuit and white heels, but now she's starting to question this decision as she grasps the handrail and a heel slips a little on the metal.

Before she can knock, the door swings open and Gust is standing there wearing a pair of fuchsia short-shorts that don't belong on a man of eighty-five, or any age at all. His chest is bare and hairless and faintly blue. "We're going swimming," he says, stepping aside to let her enter, and that's when she sees the three girls behind him. "Then we'll all bake rum cookies."

The girls are standing side by side at the kitchen counter, like barmaids in an Impressionist painting. Their piled-up hair is various shades of straw-gold; they're wearing tank tops and too much makeup. The one in the middle waves at her, and then the girls go back to whatever it is that they're doing, something that involves several bottles of liquor, a tub of vanilla ice cream, and a blender.

"Marie, Candy, and Cindy," Gust says. "Friends of my grandson's and now friends of mine."

"Rob is mad at us," says one of the girls. "So we came up here." She presses the blender and a noise like an angry monster gnashing its teeth fills the small apartment. When it stops, the girls begin pouring yellow froth into plastic tumblers. One of the girls—they all seem to have the same name—hands a tumbler over the counter to Gust and says to Hilda, "Want one?"

"No," Hilda says. She is perched on the edge of a hard green sofa, awkwardly clutching her purse and surveying her surroundings with distaste. The walls are made of cinderblock and everything smells faintly of mildew. There's a small end table, a ratty green carpet, a TV on a metal cart, and thirty or forty boxes piled against every wall. The lamp—*that* lamp—is on top of the refrigerator, as if daring her, and everyone, to look up its skirt.

Hilda feels such a surge of annoyance that she rises from the sofa and announces, "I'm just too old for this."

"You like the lamp," Gust says. "You wish you'd bought it." He takes a long drink from the tumbler and smiles at her.

"You're both so young at heart," says one of the girls, in a fake-sweet voice that, Hilda understands with a sickening lurch, is the kind of voice young people use on the elderly in nursing homes and hospitals, the voice Linda is starting to use with her, the voice Ronny (Ricky?) uses when he comes over to haul away another box she never wanted to begin with.

But Gust is grinning as if he doesn't understand any of this. As if he doesn't know that these girls are here because he's funny to them the way decrepit zoo animals are funny, and because he's giving them alcohol when they're clearly underage. She could give him a piece of her mind, tell him how foolish he seems, remind him that he's only acting this way because he isn't going to live forever.

"It's time to say good-bye," she says, in a way that seems to her very final. She clears her throat because it hasn't come out quite as strongly as she would like. In fact, he doesn't seem to have heard her at all. One of the girls is pouring a bottle of something yellow into a pitcher of something pink.

"Where's the ice?" says another girl. She smiles at Hilda. "Are you sure you wouldn't like some?"

"I would not," says Hilda. "It is time to say good-bye." *I won't be coming back, it was nice knowing you. Perhaps I will read your obituary. Perhaps you will read mine.* That would be final, wouldn't it?

"I have a lot of old books," Gust says. "I want you to take some. No charge."

"I don't have room for books," says Hilda, clutching her purse strap. "I don't have time for books. It is time to say good-bye."

Gust nods. He waggles his eyebrows and then sighs. He has a faint white mustache from the alcoholic milkshake. "Well. Let me walk you down to your car."

"You should stay up here until you're sober," she says. "So you don't trip down the steps and kiss yourself."

She knows the moment she says it that it's done, there's no taking it back. The three drunk girls have started giggling. One of them has fallen on the sofa and is snorting.

Gust says, "What's this now?" and the flash of panic on his face lets her know that he really hadn't heard her, that he doesn't understand why the girls are shaking with laughter, why one of them is saying, "Oooh, Gust. She wants to *kiss* you."

"What?" he says again. "What's so funny?" He looks at the girls, but they're giggling with increasing hilarity.

She won't blush or clamp her hand over her mouth. *Here it is*, Hilda thinks, *your housewarming gift*. She steps toward him, so close she can smell the rum on his breath. "I killed a bear once," she says, and touches her lips to the side of his face, pressing hard until she's certain that when she steps back there will be something to see.

Becky Hagenston's first collection of stories, *A Gram of Mars,* won the Mary McCarthy Prize; her second collection, *Strange Weather,* won the Spokane Prize. Twice the recipient of the O. Henry Prize, she has won many other awards. She is an associate professor of English at Mississippi State University, where she edits the *Jabberwock Review.*